Lainey Shea's Treasur

The Silver Beaver T

With Prequel Short Story - Baubles in Bermuda
Vickey Wollan

COPYRIGHT © 2024 VICKEY WOLLAN

The best way to stay in touch is to subscribe to her newsletter and add her email address (vickeywollanauthor@yahoo.com) to your contacts. This ensures you never miss a new book, a chance to win great prizes, or exclusive content. Visit her website vickeywollanauthor.com to subscribe.

You may also follow her on BookBub to be notified of new releases as they become available.

Learn more about Vickey Wollan at:
https://vickeywollanauthor.com

To Paul...
The best partner in life and business.
Your unwavering support feeds my creativity.
I'm so thankful to be taking this journey with you.

ACKNOWLEDGEMENTS

Thank you to all the people who helped me launch my sweet adventure romance series *Lainey Shea's Treasure Quest*. I've always written sweet contemporary romance. Originally, I wrote Christmas themed stories, but I hope my readers will also enjoy the direction I'm heading in with my archaeologist heroine, Lainey Shea.

An extra special thank you to cover artist Tamra Stickley of **Inventive Visions Art** Tamra painted this cover per my artistic request.

Contact her at tamramstickley@gmail.com to discuss your cover design, and follow her on Instagram and Facebook.

An ongoing thank you to my critique partner and author: Leah Miles. Your feedback is always helpful and incredibly valuable to me.

A special thank you goes to Emily Harmston, Editor.

First Coast Romance Writers provided more knowledge and support than I can describe. The members of this organizations are nurturing and generous beyond words. There are too many to name, but you can learn about them all at the First Coast Romance Writers website.

My family and friends provided unwavering support and encouragement. Special thanks to my beta readers: Diane and Bonnie. Thank you to my parents and sister for helping me believe that I can accomplish anything. My highest gratitude goes to my husband. He allowed me to follow my dream and gave me a boost every time I needed one. Your love is the greatest gift I've ever received.

Again, thank you so much to one and all.

Prequel Short Story
Baubles in Bermuda

Vickey Wollan

Bermuda's L. F. Wade International airport was a hive of activity. Helaina Shea—Lainey to her friends—grabbed her best friend, Joan, by the strap of her backpack and hauled her behind the concourse's support pillar. "Hide. Quick!"

"What the—" Regaining her balance, Joan squinted behind her intellectual-looking frames. "It's Spring Break. Why would I want to hide from anyone?"

"Be quiet," Lainey whispered. "Please." Her pulse quickened as she brought her lips to Joan's ear. "I just caught a glimpse of him—Professor Hardy. He was on our flight."

Joan's eyebrows shot up, and her body went rigid. Ever so slightly, her head dropped to one side, then she leaned in that same direction. Her motion halted when she spotted the target.

"Yep," Joan murmured as she stared. "He's got a tight tooshie."

"Excuse me?" Lainey twirled a half circle and strained to catch the same view.

"Lainey, freshman year you admitted that you sat in the front row so you could watch his derriere dance while he wrote on the blackboard. Don't deny it." She smirked and repositioned her bookbag.

After making sure he was gone, Lainey stood up straight. Throngs of people rushed past her to their destinations, heels of their shoes tapping on the tile floor. The tall windows and rows of worn seating reminded her of the many airports she'd visited. The scent of an industrial cleaning agent she could do without.

"Okay, fine." So much for Lainey's twenty-six-year-old PhD candidate sophistication. She let out a little girl giggle. "Definitely the hottest professor I've ever seen."

Joan crossed one arm over her chest and then the other. "And we're hiding why?"

"Because." Lainey pulled a scrunchy off her wrist and used it to wrangle her long mass of dark curls into a messy bun atop her head. "It's not like I'm into him. Can't a girl just enjoy the view? Besides, we're on a treasure hunt, not a manhunt."

"Can't it be both?" Joan failed at stifling a hiccup.

Lainey searched for anyone else who might know her, stepped out from her temporary concealment, and nudged Joan's arm. "Are you tipsy?"

"Those mimosas you bought us on the plane are having their effects. Blame yourself that I'm having fun. Go ahead." Joan made a beeline to the nearest restroom, and Lainey chased after her.

A short while later, with her bladder relieved, Lainey merged into the flow of scrambling people with Joan directly behind her.

Lainey suggested, "Let's hang back, check out some souvenirs, and be the last passengers to pick up our luggage."

While Joan ogled high-end jewelry and sniffed floral bouquets of pricey perfumes, Lainey admired the swimwear on a mannequin. If she were alone, she might've tried on a tiny bikini or colorful sundress, but she understood her closest confidant had no money to spare. Joan's graduate assistant salary didn't provide discretionary spending money for a vacation. So, Lainey contented herself with window shopping and enjoying her freedom from class assignment deadlines and test anxiety.

"What a lovely thing you are," a male voice said nearby.

After Joan tugged Lainey's t-shirt to get her attention, she hitched her thumb to indicate the man behind her. "You're being admired ... again."

"Huh?" Lainey caught a graceless stare from the middle-aged guy who'd spoken to her. "No, I'm not a model. Yes, I'm in an exclusive relationship."

Only the first sentence was true. She'd found it easier to fib so that gentlemen bold enough to assume she'd be interested got shot down with as little fuss as possible. Romance was way down on her to-do list. While she appreciated the fact that she'd inherited from her Buckeye faculty parents her father's height and her mother's classic features, there was more to her than that. Someday she'd be grateful for the attention, maybe, but this week she had a more pressing adventure in mind.

"Come on. The professor should've left the airport by now. Let's go to the hotel and check out the beach," said Lainey as she put additional space between herself and the unwanted admirer.

"Right behind you," chirped Joan. "Feel free to buy me a fruity rum concoction if you'd like."

The loudspeaker squawked overhead as Lainey scanned the baggage conveyors for her belongings. The sunny day brought in warmth through the windows angled over her head, and a gust of humid air wafted in every time the automatic sliding exit doors whooshed open.

"There it is." Lainey dashed to Big Red, the name she'd given her biggest suitcase, the one she'd taken on trips with her father to his archeological digs.

She'd soon be working permanently alongside her father, Dr. Michael Shea, as his assistant in the field. Assistant sounded better than lackey. Unless, of course, she could parlay her treasure hunting passion into a paying gig. She had a dream of starting a company, Shea's Treasure Seekers, to find items of value stolen or left behind, then buried and lost by the passing of time.

Bermuda had become her chosen destination to prove her three-times great grandfather's tale was more truth and less fantasy. He'd been an officer on a British Royal Navy ship. The story, passed down for generations, said pirates tried to bribe their way out of the brig by offering him a portion of the loot if he'd let them escape. Some of the descriptions were very specific. One account described the renegades offering jewels in a red velvet drawstring bag and details of the hidden location as proof. According to the verbal retellings, the leader of the miscreants had told him to look for a V-shaped landmark in the biggest cove of Bermuda.

Lainey planned to find that red velvet bag with the lady aristocrat's silver necklace, bracelet, and tiara inlaid with diamonds and emeralds. The long dead pirate had bragged that the pillage was "baubles aplenty." The description was so specific it had to be true.

Bending slightly at the knees, she jerked her bag off the conveyor belt. Then she hastened to help retrieve a similarly sized bag for Joan. The borrowed bag had belonged to Lainey's little brother, Frank, who'd passed nearly eight years prior. The pain of guilt and agony of self-doubt threatened to consume her, like it always did, when she thought of the bright, funny young man who'd died while under her care. Always energetic, Frank had stepped too quickly across scaffolding, toppling it over. A head injury ended his life. The sight of one of his belongings would forever take her breath away.

Gasping for air, Lainey placed the suitcase's wheels ever so gently on the ground as if they were her brother's feet. She pushed it toward Joan and silently vowed to embody Frank's adventurous spirit as a way of keeping a part of him with her always.

Joan stood in silence, her hand a white-knuckled grip on the handle of Lainey's brother's bag. "What's wrong?" she eventually asked. "Why'd you stop?"

"Well, will wonders never cease? Helaina Shea, is that you?"

A voice Lainey recognized called out to her from behind. She swallowed her agitation at the unwanted intrusion, plastered on an inviting smile, and turned to greet her former teacher. *I want to find the treasure on my own. I hope this is the only time I run into this guy.* "Professor Hardy, what brings you to the Bermuda?"

"The International Union of Geological Sciences' convention is always held in March. This year they picked Bermuda." He tossed back his thick blond locks and contained them under an Ohio State baseball cap. "Can I give you a lift to your hotel? Got a taxi waiting right outside."

* * *

Professor Mitch Hardy stood taller as he escorted the two beautiful ladies to the car he'd hired for the week. This was a boost to his flagging ego, having been denied tenure at the University just four weeks prior due to his "behavior." Except, he hadn't done anything wrong. Nothing in his personnel file even hinted of behavioral issues, but he hadn't figured out how to fight the unfounded excuse given for not awarding his tenure request.

Ms. Shea seemed a bit taken aback by his presence, but her friend welcomed him with a broad smile. Relieved when his former student accommodated her companion's wishes, he cheerfully waved them forward. Now he wouldn't be alone. It made him feel more important being accompanied. He adjusted his sunglasses and scolded himself to get out of his head and enjoy the tropical paradise before him.

Instead of the usual two-seater rented by tourists in Bermuda, he'd splurged on a minivan with a hired driver. He wanted to travel with a team-sized crowd tonight when his fellow conference goers went out to check out Bermuda's nightlife. After all, Mitch needed to ingratiate himself with as many geologists as possible in case he needed letters of recommendation for his second bid to acquire tenure. At least that's what he told himself.

"Bob," he asked his hired driver, "can we please drop these ladies off at their hotel before going to mine?" Mitch could only recently afford a luxury like this, and the rhetorical question helped Bob understand the change in plans.

* * *

Mitch's father had died a short nine months ago. To Mitch's surprise, his third of the estate was way more than he could have ever imagined. His older brothers were equally shocked with their portions. He guessed his old man had squirrelled away money to make himself feel more secure in what he always described as a cruel world.

Mitch's financial planner had advised him that he could retire now, at only fifty-six, and live comfortably past one hundred. For Mitch, though, the challenge of gaining tenure to earn the respect of his peers kept him working. Spending money on himself wasn't any fun. His thoughts drifted back to his chauffeured van extravagance. Could the tenure panel use it against him?

His driver popped the rear hatch and grabbed the ladies' luggage, then came back to stow Mitch's rolling bag. "Which hotel, ma'ams?" asked Bob as he hurried to open the passenger door nearest the curb.

"We're staying in a timeshare near the Bermuda Beach Club," said Ms. Shea. She slid into the middle row while he climbed into the front passenger seat.

"Perfect." Bob rounded the vehicle. Once inside, he said to Mitch, "Your hotel is within walking distance from their lodgings."

"Oh, good. We won't keep you from your busy schedule," added Ms. Shea. "My father taught me to always respect the time of my professors."

The mention of the word father sucked him back in time. He'd been the only son there for his father's last days. At least, in that, he'd received something his brothers hadn't. For a man who had never learned to show love and affection, his dad managed to hug him and tell him he was proud of what he'd accomplished in both his careers: baseball and teaching geology. His father's praise kept him grounded. Lately, he felt stuck in a frozen pond, surrounded by ice with no earthly idea how to find a source of heat.

Ms. Wagner squealed at the sight of a historical museum until Ms. Shea shushed her. He fed off their enthusiasm, and a sense of calm enveloped him.

Mitch allowed himself to grin as Bob merged into traffic onto the coastal highway where the view of the ocean reached as far as the eye could see. This trip would be the thing that put his quest for tenure over the top. He'd focus every ounce of his competitiveness into accomplishing his goal, and hopefully his good deed for the day would change his Karma in a positive direction.

LAINEY SHEA'S TREASURE QUEST: THE SILVER BEAVER TOKENS

* * *

The next morning, Lainey couldn't hold back her excitement as she hurried along a wooden dock. Gawking at the size of the boats moored in the harbor, Joan wrangled the case for the high-end metal detector, while Lainey carried her prize satchel of archeological dig tools. She had dreamed about this moment for so long and wanted to do her heritage proud.

"There it is. The Royal Explorer." Lainey picked up her pace. The forty-foot, twin inboard vessel in white with purple trim looked just like its picture. Perfect for her excursion. Even the name fit her purpose. "Hello! Permission to come aboard? It's Lainey Shea."

Joan caught up with her a bit out of breath, dropping the items she carried on the worn planks with a *thunk*. "What a beautiful day. Visibility is clear and the temperatures are bearable."

Lainey gave a quick nod as she scurried around to the other side of the slip. "Captain Peterson, are you on board?"

"No signs of life over here. Did you book the right day?" shouted Joan.

Sighing, Lainey set her bag down and pulled her cell from her back pocket. She scrolled through her emails, opening an attachment. "The contract has today's date, and I paid the deposit. We're right on time."

When she dialed the number on the email, it went straight to voicemail. Gathering her belongings, she joined Joan who'd plopped down on a nearby bench. "What's the courtesy wait time on a boat captain?"

"Need I remind you I'm a history major?"

Joan chuckled as she retrieved a bottle of diet soda from the cooler she'd recently lowered to the dock and took a swig.

The next ten minutes passed like ten hours. Several motors around them roared to life as most of the boats made their way out onto the azure water to the day's adventure. Lainey looked at the time on her phone one more time. "I have no patience for this. Let's go talk with the harbor master. Maybe he knows the whereabouts of our captain."

Having hoisted all their supplies, the trip back took much more effort. Joan was a good sport about the situation. No complaints, no dirty looks. Lainey understood what she had in this trusting and loyal friendship.

As she looked further down the dock, she noticed another traveler coming in her direction. Lainey hugged the right side of the wooden planks to make sure her oversized duffel wouldn't interfere with the fellow boater's passing.

Joan ID'd the man before she did. "Professor Hardy, if you weren't wearing your Buckeye ballcap, I wouldn't have recognized you."

Lainey stopped in her tracks and Joan, probably still admiring the view, stumbled into her. "Shouldn't you be at some presentation?" she asked.

"I'm booked all afternoon but wanted to get in some deep sea fishing this morning." Professor Hardy shifted his stance and gave her a toothy smile. "Aren't the two of you going in the wrong direction?"

Joan blurted out, "Our captain ghosted us."

Lainey gave her a disgruntled look, and her friend's shoulders drooped. "We were about to chat with the manager of the docks."

"Nonsense. It's just Bob and me this morning. There's plenty of room on the boat I hired. The captain is waiting for our return." He stepped forward and reached out to take her bag from her.

"We're not fishing." She didn't want to divulge their true intentions, but her whirling mind couldn't come up with an explanation quickly enough. She leaned away from his grasp.

His face moved through several reactions she couldn't decipher. Had she hurt his feelings or was that a flash of anger?

Bob strolled their way, hauling a huge cooler on wheels. "Ladies. So nice to see you again. Are you fishing with us?"

Joan nudged her and tilted her head in the direction of the gentlemen offering to rescue them. "Fishing isn't my thing. I want to cruise the coastline to look for a stream that empties into the sea. It's a long story."

She and Joan often took turns saving each other. Lainey's body relaxed. Joan's line of thought was straight on. She needed a boat. Digging could occur later in the week. "If you don't mind giving up fishing, we appreciate the invitation to ride."

Professor Hardy succeeded in lightening her load before she could change her mind. "You just made my day. Tell me more about this special stream."

* * *

Mitch sat next to Bob on the second row of white vinyl seating, trying to eavesdrop while his guests gave instructions to the captain about cruising the coastline. Something about going between Hamilton and Mt. Pleasant.

Being around people and not having to attend presentations on the latest research on Earth mantel striations cleared his gloomy thoughts. The fishing trip had been a great excuse to leave the conference without having folks in the geology world thinking less of him. He loved his field, but sometimes he needed to talk about something other than rocks.

Once everything fell into place and the search began, the young women removed their outer layer of clothing to catch some of the sun's rays. At first, he wouldn't let himself look, instead taking in the coconut scent of their sunscreen. Then he reminded himself that Lainey, who'd insisted he call by her nickname, was over twenty-one and no longer his student. He'd even insisted she call him Mitch.

Leaving Bob to entertain Joan, he gravitated toward the side of the boat where Lainey stood facing the beach.

With his cap on backwards and shades held in place with a sporty strap, he didn't feel middle-aged. His fifteen-year stretch as an assistant pitcher's coach had delayed him from starting his PhD in geology. During his undergrad days, he was the prank-playing teammate the coaches had to babysit while on the road.

When the job fell to him to keep young players from misbehaving, it wasn't his thing, but the coaching life had been fun while it lasted. Luckily, teaching the entry level geology class came naturally to him. Most of the students who enrolled in the class had earned sports scholarships. Having lived it, he spoke their language and treated each one of them like a valued individual.

Mitch surveyed Lainey from her adorable toes, up her irresistible curves, all the way to her perky nose. Her wide-brimmed hat only partially inhibited her long hair from blowing freely in the wind. Falling into a daydream of her on his arm at faculty events, he had to shake his head to clear the vision. He needed to stay focused on his career goal—tenure.

"What's so important about this stream?" He handed Lainey his binoculars, feeling the warmth of her skin as their hands slid past each other.

"You brought these to fish?" she asked, having immediately raised them to her dark eyes.

"Oh, I'm a bit of a Boy Scout. Always be prepared. It's the only way I had any hope of beating my two older brothers at anything." The sound of him continuing the conversation startled her away from her focus on the beach. He grinned when he realized she hadn't expected an answer but let him know she'd heard his response by smiling.

"Can we make another pass of the same area?" asked Lainey. More like directed him. He didn't mind.

"Sure." He went to the steering console and politely asked the captain to hug the coast as close as he dared. Then he hurried back, anxious to be near her. He realized he was no longer able to deny his attraction to his former student.

She remained engrossed with her task and hadn't sensed his return, so he enjoyed her beauty as she intently scrutinized the coast. Finally, he mustered the courage to ask, "Have dinner with me tonight?" He quickly corrected himself. "I'd like to take you and Joan out to dinner tonight, please."

He couldn't miss Joan's face whipping in his direction, and he had to bite the inside of his cheek to keep from laughing at Lainey's utter surprise.

"Don't you have plans with the rock people?" Lainey choked out.

Mitch kept his tone even. "Tomorrow, yes. Dinner is on our own tonight. I want to try the Majestic Seafood & Chophouse. I hear they have the best sushi."

"Joan loves sushi," Lainey said.

"That's a fact." Joan sidestepped closer to them. "We can accept Professor Hardy's generosity. How about it?"

"We'll think about it." Lainey's gaze once again became glued to where the water met the sand.

Mitch checked the time. "I must be back at the conference by one. If we eat lunch on the boat, we'll have time for another pass of this cove."

With a quick nod, Lainey went back to searching. "Save mine for later," she said.

So, he offered Joan a cold cut sandwich and glass of fruit punch which she eagerly drank.

He leaned on the rail and allowed himself to enjoy the salty ocean air and glorious view of Bermuda and Lainey. "At dinner, you can tell me more about the importance of this stream. Geologically speaking, maybe I can help."

* * *

Lainey frowned sympathetically at her friend. "Oh, my goodness. It must be something you ate. You never get sick." Compassion overflowed as Joan stumbled back to bed after another run to the restroom.

Her friend pulled a pillow over her head. "Go. Go without me. Enjoy a fancy meal at the swankiest eatery on the island. Ugh. Just don't tell me anything about the food." She wrapped her arms around her tummy, then bolted back into the bathroom.

Lainey leaned against the wall, the tropical-patterned wallpaper entirely too cheerful considering the woman praying for death on the other side of the door. "Are you sure?"

"Yes. You have time to buy a new dress if you hurry." A flushing sound muffled the rest of Joan's words.

"Text me if you need anything. Feel better." Lainey glanced down at her more comfortable than fashionable outfit and sighed. She didn't need girly clothes on a dig for treasure. That's what she'd told herself while packing. Tonight was only a platonic meal, but a stylish new dress would highlight having dinner at a five-star restaurant. Grabbing her handbag, she made her way down to the shop in the hotel lobby.

One dress in particular called to her from the shop's window every time she passed, a little black number in satin with sequined spaghetti straps. Luckily, they had one on the rack in a size eight. After a flurry in the dressing room, Lainey made her way to a three-paneled mirror.

"No one's worn it better," said a shop employee.

The clerk behind her, visible in the mirror's reflection, held a strappy pair of stilettos with sparkling accents that matched the sophisticated frock. Trying to not reveal her excitement, she gave the woman her shoe size. In minutes, she'd transformed from a playful college co-ed to a glamorous woman.

With the purchases made and tags off, Lainey strode with as much speed as her new heels would allow back to her room. She tossed her old clothes on the bed and twisted her hair into a loose up-do with the most decorative barrette in her carry-on. Adding a swipe of rosy lip gloss, she approved of her appearance with a nod.

Then she headed downstairs to wait for Professor Hardy. She was early, so she walked out beside the immaculately landscaped circle drive, allowing herself to people watch. After a few minutes, she realized she was the person receiving attention. Embarrassed at first because she rarely dressed up, she figured it was the exquisite ensemble, not the body in it. But her smile grew with every head, turning to stare.

When the professor's van pulled up, his inelegant jaw drop caused heat to grow on her cheeks. He stepped out and offered his hand as if to help Cinderella into her carriage for the ball.

"You clean up well. Please, forgive my Neanderthal lack of manners as I approached." He tugged on his collar. "I'd have worn a tie if I'd known you'd go all out."

She thought he looked more than amazing down to his well-polished dress shoes. *Was that gel keeping his hair in place?* "You look fine. You got my text, right? Joan's under the weather."

"Sorry to hear it. We can manage just the two of us. Bob will drop us at the door of the Majestic Seafood & Chophouse and stay with the rental."

The strength of his grasp and the grace of his movement as he assisted her into the seat had her stomach fluttering. Just another meal with faculty. She'd done it with her parents hundreds of times. No big deal. Except something seemed different. She couldn't put her finger on what.

At the restaurant, the maître d' led them to a table for two. Rusty orange and hazy yellow beams of the setting sun provided a gorgeous view as they danced across rolling ocean waves. The opulent wooden furniture was well accented with plush cushions, and the ceiling-to-floor drapes made the ambience of the place live up to its reputation. It was the fanciest eatery she'd ever seen. There was a vase on the table filled with vibrantly colored flowers. She brought it to her nose for a lengthy whiff.

"May I order us a bottle of wine?" asked the professor with a gleam in his eye she didn't know how to categorize.

"Sure. And since I'm a landlocked girl, go ahead and order sushi for me, too." Her feminist leanings had never let a male order her food, but she thought it might be fun to see if she liked being pampered by a distinguished man more versed in life's experiences.

"Of course. While we're at it, beyond using first names, please don't think of me as your former professor." His blue eyes met hers as if he dared her to gaze back without breaking their connection.

So, she did. His laugh lines suited him, and he didn't look his age. The sommelier brought the bottle Mitch had masterfully requested. *Where did Mr. Baseball learn how to be a well-polished gentleman?* The man in front of her was both athletic and intellectual. She decided to allow herself to enjoy this rare combination of gifts. Every piece of sushi she ate had her tastebuds asking for more, and the savory couscous melted on her tongue.

"Let's address the elephant in the room." She'd been thinking it but shocked herself when the words spilled from her mouth.

He steepled his index fingers and leaned in. "I'm listening."

"My parents agreed, not that they'd admit it outside of their living room. You got a raw deal. You deserve tenure as much as anyone in the geology department. And I concur." She sipped the dry Chablis and let her pinky float a bit higher.

His hard swallow was visible as he sat back in his chair. "Very kind of you to say. Unfortunately, your esteemed opinions don't change what happened."

The tension in his body made her want to comfort him. "Let's break it down. Why'd you fail and how can you do better next time?"

The servers inconspicuously brought and removed dishes while they talked.

"I can't change who's on the committee. A couple of tenured professors seem to have it out for me." Adept at using chopsticks, he picked up a piece of sushi and dipped it in sauce before popping it to his mouth in one big bite. "I get good teaching reviews," he said a few moments later. "The textbook I wrote didn't break sales records, but it's profitable."

"How did your book sales compare to other geology professors on the committee? Are your reviews better?"

"Oh, I hadn't thought of that. My best review said my entertaining descriptions made a dry topic more engaging for today's learning styles." He reached into the front pocket of his dinner jacket and pulled out his phone. A few clicks later, he dropped his cell onto the table. "You're onto something. Okay, smarty, what else have you got? It's not like throwing that in their faces will help my chances."

Pausing, she glanced over the dessert menu. "This may be tough for you to hear."

He raised both hands and snapped his fingers. "Presto, I've got my coat of armor on. Hit me."

13

Lainey couldn't help but smile at his reaction and openness to her opinion. "I bet they're jealous that you're a good-looking athlete turned scholar. And you might party a little too much." She wondered if the half bottle of wine had gone to her head. She sat up straighter and took stock of her composure.

"I enjoy viewing sporting events with groups of people. It's not like I stay out late drinking too much every day. Speaking of enjoying life, I'm in the mood for cognac and baked Alaska. You game?" His eyebrows did a mischievous twitch.

All she could do was nod. She'd never seen this side of him, but she liked it more than expected. After the dessert order had been placed, he twisted his napkin and dropped his gaze to his lap. She reached out, took his hand, and gave it a brief squeeze.

Without looking up, he continued. "Please, allow me to elaborate more on my so-called partying ways. Everybody knows I have a no drugs policy. I've never served alcohol to underaged students, and I pay for the Ubers to get my guests home safe as needed."

"Do you invite them?" she asked.

"Who? The people in my department? Of course."

"Have they ever attended?"

"No." The volume raised in his answer, the tension in his face visible.

"Can you change that?"

His response came as a whisper, and every part of him drooped as if he'd given up hope. "I doubt it."

Her rapid-fire questions ended when the server came to create the baked Alaska as a tableside show. It was like Mitch put a box around his emotions and sealed it with a fancy bow. He changed the subject to the beauty of the sunset and spoke about the conference lectures. He had to be worried, a teaching career without tenure, but it seemed he no longer wanted his troubles to mar their evening. She enjoyed sipping cognac and his companionship. This wasn't a date, but if it were, she'd describe it as the best one she'd had in years.

He surprised her again when he angled toward her to ask, "The night is young. Will you take a walk on the beach with me?"

She couldn't think of a reason to say no, and she loved to walk on the beach. "Honestly, that sounds like a wonderful idea. But Joan—"

"You can speak to Ms. Wagner to see how she's feeling. I won't be offended."

* * *

Mitch studied Lainey's long legs as she stepped out onto the deck to call her friend. The curve of her calves put thoughts into his mind that hadn't been there in a while. He'd sworn off romance when his ex told him she'd married him to get back at her father, the coach of his baseball team. *Who did that?* He'd done the honorable thing and kept the divorce amicable, though the parting words of his ex-wife still drove a knife in his heart today. She'd "never loved him." Maybe Lainey could pull out the dagger and help him to heal? No one had discussed his tenure issue with such honesty and helpful intention.

When he looked up to see her walking toward him, her perky cleavage became his focus, and he sucked in a breath. His companion this evening had more than beauty. Her compassion and understanding of people's motivations drew him to her more than he wanted. *She is worth possible heartbreak.* He led her to the van near the beach and told Bob he could take a well-deserved thirty-minute break.

"Let's leave our shoes in the van." He opened the hatch, took off his jacket, then careful to fold it, laid it over the headrest of the back seat and yanked off his shoes and socks. As his heartrate quickened, Mitch helped her get seated and bent to work on the buckles at her ankles.

"I'm ticklish."

He did his best to hide a lusty grin. "I can't guarantee I won't sneak a peek when you bend over in that dress."

She snickered and covered her plump lips with a delicate hand. "Fine. I'll try not to squirm."

As he caressed her soft skin his agile fingers worked their magic. Dangling the pair by their straps, he flung the heels onto the carpet in the storage area of the rental.

Holding his breath, he held out his hand, and when she took it, he smiled so wide his face hurt. "My turn to say something I've wanted to say for a long time," he uttered, glancing in her direction as he guided her onto the cool sand.

"That's only fair."

He liked that her long strides kept pace with his. That didn't happen often. He laced his fingers with hers. "It wasn't your fault. I wanted to tell you when

I attended Frank's memorial, but that was before you took my class. Instead, I mentioned it to your parents at a faculty event."

He turned his gaze at the waves rushing up to his feet. *Maybe I've overstepped my bounds.* "Since it's your Spring Break that's all I'm going to say about the matter. If you ever want to talk about it, though, I'm here for you." He wasn't certain where his honesty came from, but having made the statement caused a bit of warmth to gather around the block of ice that caged him and threatened his happiness.

"I miss Frank every day. Lots of people say it wasn't my fault. I can't bring myself to believe them," she said quietly as she stared out across the water.

When Lainey fell silent, he figured he'd messed up like he always did with women. He halted and tilted his head up to view the stars, and she did the same without letting go of his hand.

"I feel him watching over me. It's like he whispers in my ear to be courageous and chase my dreams."

She didn't seem emotional. Quite the opposite. So, he let her talk. When she finished telling a few funny stories about Frank, he started strolling again. "The reason you came to Bermuda, this quest of yours. Tell me about it."

He hoped his redirection of the subject wasn't too obvious. Maybe it was the breezy night air or the alcohol, but Lainey opened up more to him than she had at dinner. The tales of her three-times great-grandfather as an officer in the British Royal Navy were as entertaining as they were intriguing.

"Did you bring the treasure map with you?" he asked.

"It's not a map, and I brought a replica. My dad has the original under an airtight seal."

"See? You're so smart. I'd have brought the original and ruined it for sure." He meant the compliment wholeheartedly.

"Well, I've been under my father's wing ever since I can remember. You have a mentor for geology, right? Someone to guide you?"

His toes dug into the sand as he came to a stop again, and he took a long moment to ponder the question. "Not really. My father was a carpenter. When I switched after coaching baseball for fifteen years to get my PhD in geology, I had the impression no one took me seriously."

"That's too bad. Is there anyone in geology you look up to? Maybe they can help you earn tenure."

Her questions were innocent and yet so poignant.

"I'm going to say something," he said, "and I hope I don't choose the wrong words."

"I'll give you a hall pass. Out with it." She turned and faced him.

"You have an old soul. You're more mature than me." He wanted to drag her into his arms and hold her close but resisted the urge. "Not to say that you're old or that I'm immature."

She made a timeout sign in front of his face, and he managed to relax. "After the accident, my parents wouldn't let me be alone. I ended up spending way more time with adults than people my age. I guess that experience gave me a broader perspective. And I don't consider you immature."

She laughed lightly, and it sent another blast of heat to melt his frozen existence. What was happening? What power did this woman have to help him? "You get me. I'm enjoying our time together so much. Can I hug you?" He'd blurted out the words but didn't want to take them back.

"Ah—" she began.

Mitch could only interpret the expression that crossed her face as one of shock. He hastened a step back, then another to the side before he continued his walk toward the last glimmers of sunlight. She hadn't continued at his side. *So much for considering this a date.* He gave himself an imaginary thwack in the back of the head. Probably deserved worse.

"I didn't say no," she called from behind.

When he glanced over his shoulder to see her arms raised in offer of a hug, a thrill went through his body. His knees knocked as he made his way back to her. The hug was sublime. He dared to pull her closer and nuzzle his nose into her floral scented curls, a slight tremble in his hands as she leaned into him. A fire ignited within him to thaw his self-imposed icy purgatory.

"I want to kiss you," he spoke softly, moving his mouth as close to her ear as he dared.

She shifted back, and he lowered his chin to his chest, thinking she would pull away.

When she threaded her fingers around his neck and hauled his lips to hers, he thought he'd break instead of bend. Then he realized she'd gone up on her toes to bridge the gap, and it was too late. Her warm, moist lips brushed against his. With a quick gasp of air, he unleashed his inner need. Nipping, sucking, then teasing, gliding, and exploring, his lips found a version of heaven on earth.

She moaned.

It sent him over the edge into a chasm of pleasure. As if flamethrowers had come at him from all sides, his pitiful existence became an inhabitable chilly cave. He sensed the opening, and his mind moved toward it. Hope was within reach.

An annoying sound interrupted the spell between them. Then it happened again.

"My phone. Sorry, it might be Joan." She pulled free of his embrace.

Every cell in his brain screamed. An avalanche followed by a swiftly moving glacier kept him from freedom, but he'd managed to hold onto the hope.

"Joan is asking for an electrolyte drink." Her freshly kissed mouth turned downward. "That was … I mean I liked … but we need to go slowly. Very slowly." She turned and walked toward the van.

His feet wouldn't move. He shouted, "We can use the boat I hired again in the morning."

"Let's see how Joan is tomorrow. I feel bad that I left her alone tonight." The distance between them grew.

With an awkwardness unlike his athletic self, he chased after her.

* * *

The next morning, Lainey looked over at Joan still in bed. "We can continue the search tomorrow if you're not up to it."

Joan rolled over and threw the quilted covers off. Slowly, she propped herself up on one elbow. "If you don't mind me being a little slow, I'm game to go."

"On a boat with no food in your stomach?"

"Yeah, a shower should do the trick. Can you bring me some bland food? Please …" Her pal gave her a sad puppy dog look, then stumbled toward the bathroom.

Lainey had a continental breakfast all set up on their tiny balcony by the time Joan finished dressing. A dewy breeze blew as the sun began its climb into the sky. She wiped her mouth with a napkin and found herself preoccupied with her lips. Mitch could kiss a girl senseless. He'd made her feel special and listened, really listened to her all night. Maybe older men were better at it because of the added experience?

"I have a confession to make," said Joan before taking a small bite of dry toast.

Lainey stifled a laugh. "What kind of trouble did you get yourself into last night of all nights?"

"I needed something to occupy my brain, so I cyberstalked Mitch." She looked out at the sea.

"I can't imagine you found much dirt on him." Lainey stuffed the rest of her muffin into her mouth and began to clean up the food wrappers.

"No. It struck me that he didn't make it into Major League Baseball because he had pitch control consistency issues, then it didn't work out for him as a coach. Soon after his mom died, he switched careers. Now, he didn't earn tenure. That's gotta bruise a guy's ego." She picked up her toast. "I'm just saying ...."

Lainey stopped clearing the table, a heaviness growing in her chest. "Nothing has come easy for him, that's for sure. Do you think I'm taking advantage of him for letting us use the boat he hired?"

"Oh, about that. I found a map of the waterways throughout the island." Joan turned her laptop toward Lainey, then laid the replica of the squiggly line next to it. The paper flapped in the wind before she could contain it. "None of them match."

Lainey sighed.

"Maybe we should switch to a land excursion today. I'm not just saying that because the thought of being at sea makes me queasy," added Joan.

Patting her pal on the shoulder, Lainey stood to clear the trash and checked the time. She'd texted Mitch to confirm she'd meet him on the dock this morning. "Let's let Mitch, the captain, and Bob have a look at the sketch of the creeks. If they can't take us directly to it, then it's land ho."

* * *

After the bad news email Mitch had just read, the text he'd received from Lainey brightened his day. He allowed himself to enjoy the view as she strolled down the wooden planks. He wanted to give her a quick peck, even if it were just on the cheek but had decided to treat her like a colleague. *Business this morning, more pleasure tonight.*

"We may not need the boat after all," called out Lainey. "Let me show the lot of you something."

Mitch was the last to take a seat around a tiny fold out surface in the captain's cabin. The sight of the sheet of paper protected in a gallon-sized freezer bag had his pulse racing. *Finding this treasure could be my chance. My chance to prove myself and gain tenure.*

"So, unless you know where this body of water is, I think our search should switch to land," said Lainey, finishing her presentation.

The captain looked at Bob, then at him and shook his head.

Bob shrugged.

"Geologically speaking," Mitch said, "it's been so long since the pirates drew that line, the stream could have changed course enough that it wouldn't look the same today. Can you tell us everything else you know about the treasure's legend?" He held his breath.

"Can I have a word, Mitch? In private, please." Lainey gathered her papers and made her way off the boat.

Those words never meant anything good, especially coming from a woman. He strode into her personal space and whispered in her ear. "Last night was great. I'd be more than happy to help you on land."

She leaned back. He nearly stumbled as he recentered himself. Her sheepish smile gave him hope, but then she took two full steps in retreat. A lump formed in his throat.

"I had a wonderful time with you." She paused and closed her eyes.

This can't be good.

"For me, this trip and the hunt is about Frank more than anything else. Of all my relatives, Frank wanted to seek this treasure the most. Based on the painting in my father's study, he even looked like our three-times great grandfather reborn. I'm trying to finish what Frank started." One side of her mouth created a lopsided smile, but then she grew serious again.

"I'm trying to find closure. Being happy with you wouldn't work as it should while I'm processing my grief. I hope you understand."

It was like a heavy-weight boxer punched him in the gut. He fixed a stoic expression on his face, one well-practiced from frequent use over the years. Lainey had put the possibility of a romance between them out of his reach.

"Yes, of course. I'm here if you need anything, anything all at." As he stood bathed by the glow of the sun on a cloudless day, his entire world became a frozen tundra once more.

"After I put his ghost to rest for good, I'll see you back on campus. Okay?"

He had to act like she didn't affect him, so he cleared his throat and said, "I reached out to a potential mentor like you suggested." His voice cracked. "He politely turned me down. Then he added that all the tenured geology professors already had mentees."

"That was rude."

The wind blew through Lainey's curls. He wanted to gather a handful of her hair to his nose once more, but it wouldn't be appropriate with the rest of the group nearby.

"You understand if I don't get tenure on my second try, I'll be encouraged to resign. Albeit unofficially. So, no. I may not see you on campus or anywhere else." Keeping his eyes to the ground, he boarded the boat and entered the small captain's cabin without a backwards glance.

* * *

Lainey's trusty sidekick raced in her direction off the dock onto the beach, hauling the archaeology gear with a grimace.

"What was that about?" asked Joan.

"I can't think of romance now. Even if he is a really good kisser." Lainey's posture hunched.

"Wait ... what?"

"I don't want to talk about it right now. Can we please concentrate on using the metal detector in the "V" area near Hamilton?" Lainey asked.

As best friends know to do, Joan dropped the subject and instead assembled the machines. Lainey kept avoiding eye contact until she conjured a plan for the rest of the day. Perhaps the tale about the bejeweled treasure passed through the generations was a hoax? One more big push on land, she told herself, giving herself a pep talk. "If we don't find a clue, we can party and sunbathe the rest of Spring Break."

Lainey pointed out landmarks to Joan. "Let's make a sweep of the beach and the shoreside park at the narrowest part of this bay. We can reassess our progress in an hour or two."

With sweat rolling down her back, she walked a straight line, waving the wand and hoping to hear a beep, then she took one side step and walked parallel to her first path. She'd taught Joan the same technique so they could efficiently cover more ground. At one point, she recalibrated her equipment. The defiant contraption remained disappointingly silent.

A damp, discolored, empty money clip didn't count as treasure. Everything she dug up from the sand went straight into a bag for trash she'd strapped over her shoulder. Ignoring the strange looks she received as people staked out a plot of land for their oversized umbrellas and blankets, she finished the square she'd assigned to herself and went to help Joan complete her quadrant.

"Find anything noteworthy?" asked Lainey with a drooping smile.

Joan let out a burst of forced laughter, then shook her head. "My cheers of joy would have echoed to you from my side of the beach."

Lainey looked at the time on her cell and sighed. "Let's find some shade and take a water break."

Sitting on a rock under a palm tree, she took a full circle view of her surroundings. Who knew what this spot looked like in the 1850s? With so many buildings and roads, the treasure could be buried deeper or paved over. When she went to excavation sites with her father, the hard part of finding where to dig had already been accomplished. *Maybe teaching is more my calling than field work. Where's my patience to keep trying?*

"I have an idea," offered Joan.

Startled by the intrusion into her thoughts, she gave Joan a wide-eyed look.

"You're not going to like it."

Lainey wanted to roll her eyes but gave Joan a playful shove instead. "What?"

"I say we go to one of the forts. You know take in some historical landmarks like you promised." Joan flashed her a toothy grin.

"That's a wonderful idea. I'm game." Lainey leapt to her feet, yanking Joan up with her.

LAINEY SHEA'S TREASURE QUEST: THE SILVER BEAVER TOKENS

* * *

Per Joan's request, Lainey found herself entering Fort George. When her bestie purchased the tourist guide for the historic British military fortress, she recognized the significance of this trip. Following Joan like a well-behaved service dog, she read the plaques and made sure Joan had time to study every noteworthy artifact.

"Look! The re-enactors are here today, and we're in time for the cannon firing," squealed Joan as she ran out to the farthest point of the stone half-wall facing the ocean.

Oh, joy. Not. But Joan had had it rough last night and still scrounged up enough energy to sprint, so Lainey trotted after her. Why a girly girl was into cannons Lainey didn't understand. Every word of the artillery officer in his historically accurate British red, black, and gold uniform was taken in with utmost interest. Lainey enjoyed Joan's behavior more than the show. After the cannon went off and the boom caused a bit of ringing in her ears, it pleased her to hang back while Joan continued her exploration.

"Come over here, Lainey." Joan motioned for her. "They're not gonna fire this one any time soon. Look, it's got a big crack in it." She nudged her closer to the mouth of the iron barrel.

Everything fell away as Lainey's focus lasered in the on the crooked pattern of the crack. The shape had been etched into her mind. No need to pull out the replica drawing.

"That's it!" Lainey screamed with a volume that jarred even her nerves. She feathered her index finger along the fissure in the hard metal, then scurried to thrust her arm into the circular hole.

"It's too long. I can't reach all the way to the back."

Beside her, Joan did a dab move, making her arms into a lightning bolt. "I get it. The line wasn't a stream. It's the crack in the cannon."

Other tourists began to gather round. The artillery officer came running.

"Ma'am, please remove your arm. That's not a toy," he commanded.

Lainey did as asked but ignored the growing hubbub. She turned to Joan. "I'm a pirate being chased by the law. No time to dig a hole. This cannon is a perfect hiding place."

"With that crack, it wouldn't be in service. It'd probably be in the scrap heap. Historically speaking." Joan sounded like the professor she'd soon become.

"Grab a piece of parchment and coal, or dirt even, to trace the crack to create the drawing we know wasn't a map. Brilliant." Lainey's palms were clammy, and her mind whirled. *How am I going to get to the base of the cannon?*

She grasped the forearm of the officer who'd been watching nervously. "I need to speak to the person in charge of this installation right away. Joan, go get my dig tools. Hurry, while we still have daylight."

"Has this cannon been here since the building of the fort?" asked Joan, holding up a finger at Lainey.

The officer freed himself from Lainey's grasp. "Between you and me, not necessarily. After the Historical Society chose which landmarks to make into museums, all the artifacts of the island were brought to those locations."

Joan continued her inquisition. "So, this cannon could have been in the cove near Hamilton?"

"It's possible," he replied.

Lainey went back to the barrel's opening. "Good. I need to see what's inside this thing."

The officer thrust himself bodily in between the Lainey and the cannon. "You'll do no such thing."

* * *

Mitch couldn't believe it when the news reached him. He'd been in the middle of a presentation on shifting sedimentation under glaciers and walked right out.

The first night he'd been in Bermuda, his reminisces about the good ole days as a pitcher while at the bar had drawn a crowd, especially since he bought the last round. Luckily, some of the people listening to his stories had been local politicians.

Now, as if he'd brought the cavalry, he marched into Fort George with several elected officials who had authority in tow. The sight of Lainey pleading her case with some guy in a military uniform and the rest of the folks in business attire put wind in his sails. *Will she give me a second chance? Have I done enough?*

"Lainey," Mitch called out to her over the din. "This is Mr. Wadsworth. Tell him what you need. He can overrule the fort's director."

Her eyes grew wide at the sight of him. "What are you doing here?"

His mouth went dry as his throat constricted. She didn't look pleased to see him. All he could think to do was step back and let the local officials argue it out. Staying hidden in the crowd, he strained to hear each person as they spoke.

Mr. Wadsworth took center stage, wagging his finger at the museum staff. "I'll take this clear to the Governor if I must. She's a trained archaeologist. Her proposed course of action won't hurt the cannon. If there are jewels in there, think of the benefit to Bermuda."

Out of the corner of his eye, Mitch witnessed Joan with two heavy duffels, one heaved over each shoulder, get held back by the growing crowd. He wanted to go help her but couldn't tear himself from away from the pull Lainey had over him. For the first time since he'd walked away from her this morning, the ache in his chest had subsided.

Lainey asked, "Do I have the go ahead?"

* * *

In the now crowded area in the corner of the fort where the flawed cannon sat, Lainey got in the parliamentarian's face and asked again. "Do you have the authority to grant me access to the inside of the cannon?"

In his expensive suit, Mr. Wadsworth took a moment to wipe his brow in the heat of the afternoon sun and made eye contact with specific people. "Cordon off the area. No one should be within one hundred yards without my permission."

Most people withdrew as requested and a few folks approached, including Professor Hardy. She wanted to delve into how he managed to find out about the situation but had more pressing priorities.

Before Lainey could begin her work, Mr. Wadsworth held up his hand like a stop sign. Retrieving his cell, he scrolled through his contacts and dialed. "Thank goodness I caught you. Can you bring your mobile x-ray unit to Fort George today, like right now? I'll explain when you arrive."

Then, Wadsworth hovered near Lainey and whispered in low tones so only she could hear. "I hope you're right about the jewels. My friend at the Bermuda

Electric Light Company is bringing his non-destructive testing equipment to confirm if there are objects in the cannon before you go poking around down the barrel."

All Lainey could do was nod. "That's a great idea. I didn't pack anything like that in my luggage."

"He's on his way. It'll be just a few moments." He went back to crowd control.

"Joan's with me. Please, allow her to come forward." Lainey gave her pal a big grin when she finally got through the throng and lowered the heavy bags at Lainey's feet.

"What'd I miss?"

"We're on pause until the mobile x-ray unit arrives." Lainey began to organize what she expected to use, then paced the length of the cannon, pivoted, and repeated the movement.

Her heart jumped into her throat when a bald guy in grey coveralls carrying a heavy rectangle case approached Mr. Wadsworth. She strained to hear but couldn't. How could she have come so far just to be told to wait on the sidelines? Her head throbbed.

The workman knelt and set up his monitor then ran a probe along the circumference of the base of the cannon several time. As the man glanced at the screen, Lainey inched closer, peering over his shoulder.

"After the solid mass, it looks there are a bunch of air pockets deeper down the cylinder," she offered, startling the safety expert.

The electric company employee rose and directed his findings at Mr. Wadsworth. "I'm with her. Either someone did a bad job of packing this cannon or there's something else in there."

The man in the coveralls quickly stepped aside, hovering in the front row of onlookers, but not before Lainey nearly shook his arm off with her exuberant expression of gratitude.

After conveying his thanks to his friend, Mr. Wadsworth patted the cannon. "She's all yours."

Lainey went into commander mode. "Can someone get me a table and tray with a lip on it like you'd find in the cafeteria." Grasping a flashlight, she aimed the beam down the shaft of the cannon's barrel.

"Take a look. What's blocking my view?" She handed off the Maglite to her friend, now field assistant.

Joan knelt and shined the beam from every exterior angle available to her. "Looks like grapeshot or case shot to me. It's a cluster of small shrapnel-filled metal balls, and that's good for us. We can break through the rusty spots."

The requested items arrived, and Lainey scurried about placing her drop cloth on the tray. She set up bags to capture less important pieces and one for the jewelry she sought. With a long finely pointed poker, she aimed along the sides of the inner barrel, making a circular perforated line. Before she finished, portions of the grapeshot gave way.

Everyone around her noticed her progress and grew closer, but Professor Hardy physically kept them at bay with his arms thrown wide. "She's a professional. Give her space to work."

Lainey kept her eyes forward, a grin playing at the edges of her mouth. *He's helped or protected me every step of the way. He's a good guy. I can trust him.*

Using a long-handled claw like a disabled person would use to get a can off a shelf they couldn't reach, Lainey pulled out piece after piece of the case shot. Her next breath inhaled some particles of iron rust. The taste reminded her of blood, so she reached for a protective mask and eye goggles. After a painstakingly slow and meticulous removal of unrecognizable metal objects, one came out with a bit of red dust mixed with fine pieces of rust. She hooted and hollered from behind her protective gear.

"That's got to be from the red velvet bag. It doesn't surprise me that it's disintegrated after all these years, even protected behind the cannon fodder."

"Smart thinking of the pirates to put the grapeshot in after the bag. Better hiding place," said Joan, handing Lainey the turkey baster, so she could puff air over objects to remove dust as they were freed from their hiding place.

As she continued removing the cannon's contents, they became larger and larger. Soon, whole pieces of the damaged material and golden rope came forth.

Using the light beam once more, a sparkle flashed back at her. *I did it. The legend is real.* With a shaky hand and racing heart, she repositioned the claw. It seemed to have grasped onto something larger than shrapnel. She gave it a gentle tug. The sound of something scraping against the cast iron unnerved her. Just for a moment. Hopefully, what was left of the velvet would protect the silver and precious stones.

Lifting the claw up a tiny bit reduced the friction, she slowly backed away from the round mouth of the cannon. A second step, then a third. Finally, a cluster of tarnished silver cleared the cast iron to freedom. With gloved hands, fine bristled brushes, and her turkey baster, she cleaned and separated the items of jewelry. Just as the pirates had claimed, a matching tiara, necklace, and bracelet studded with emeralds and diamonds appeared.

Time stood still. Lainey wasn't sure if she'd been breathing. Her mind became a cluttered jumble of thoughts about her three-times-great-grandfather, her father, and most importantly, of Frank. Having met her goal for his benefit lifted some of the guilt she'd carried. His spirit had guided her. She hoped Frank could now rest in peace. The way she would remember him took a more uplifting turn, and a tear of joy rolled down her cheek.

There was a loud clap, followed by a round of hands meeting, which became a thunderous roar, which drew her attention back to the present. Professor Hardy had started the applause to provide the acclaim she had earned.

"Anybody know a good jeweler? These need a professional cleaning before we go public with the news of the find." Lainey laughed out loud, and everyone joined in.

"May I have a private word?" Professor Hardy put his palm on the small of her back and guided her to the edge of the fort, away from the chatter.

"Can you make it quick? I'm kinda busy here."

* * *

Mitch took a long moment to choose the proper words while she removed her protective facial covering. He looked deep into her brown eyes. She didn't look away. It gave him courage. Easing closer, he combed his fingers through her tendrils of curls.

"You're the best thing that has entered my life in a long time, and I wanted to be the first to congratulate you. I'm so glad you were able to do this for yourself and your brother. I hope it brings you all the success in the world."

"You've been incredibly helpful since I arrived in Bermuda." Before she could continue, several other onlookers encircled her, vying for her attention.

Mitch eased back to allow her to shine in the victory of her accomplishment. She'd earned that much.

"We'll talk more later," she called to him over the tangle of voices.

* * *

That evening Lainey sat with Joan in the condo. Her exhausted body lay still while her mind raced on a grand prix-style rollercoaster. The terrible image of falling scaffolding began to fade, instead being replaced by all the good times she and Frank had spent together. The dreams of how this discovery would help launch her treasure hunting career, however, kept getting replaced with her walk on the beach with Mitch. And that glorious kiss. She wanted a repeat performance.

The view of Joan sprawled on a chair brought her back to the present. "I couldn't have done this without you. Can I list you as a historical consultant and field assistant?"

Joan sprung into an elongated seated position that Miss Manners herself would be proud of. "That would be awesome. You're so generous and kind."

"I'm thinking about giving Mitch partial credit for the find."

Joan's jaw dropped, and she went limp again. "It's not a geology find. How would that help his situation?"

Lainey sighed. "You're right."

"Wait a minute." Joan rushed across the room and flopped next to her on the couch. "You've fallen for him, haven't you?"

Lainey looked away and searched her heart for the answer.

"You have! It's written all over your face. So exciting."

"If I help him get his tenure, he'll still be on campus. I can take my time to see if this is real or a Spring Break fling."

"Fine. Take it slow. Blah, blah, blah." Joan scooched up to place her head on a pillow. "What he needs is publicity."

"You're so brilliant. That's perfect. I can list him as a field assistant and let him speak at the press conference." Butterflies fluttered in her stomach at the thought of sharing a stage with Mitch.

* * *

29

The following afternoon, Lainey found herself in a private area of Bermuda's Government House preparing to enter the press room. She'd called her parents with the good news. They agreed it wouldn't hurt her career if she let Professor Hardy have a speaking part during the reward ceremony, but it should be her decision. Of course, she didn't mention the romantic dinner or steamy kiss between them.

She'd taken Joan on a shopping spree to buy each of them both skirt suits for the press conference. Lainey laughed to herself that she should have thought to pack one but loved having the excuse to purchase something for her roommate to thank her for understanding of cannons.

The call she made to Mitch letting him know she'd allow him to participate in today's announcement as a field assistant had been more enjoyable than she'd imagined. She expected him to say thank you. Instead, he showered her with compliments about how much he appreciated her and respected her on a variety of levels.

The press correspondents sat in theater style rows on the edge of their seats as a line of news cameras filled the outer walkway. She'd seen similar events on television but never imagined she'd be the person everyone came to see.

With her curls restrained in a tight bun at her nape, in a fully buttoned up white blouse, and the shimmer of her polyblend grey suit, she took center stage. Accepting the certificate of appreciation and finder's fee check from the Governor was the easy part. Then the photos of the jewels flashed onto the screen behind her, and the excitement level in the room rose to a fevered pitch.

She tried to quiet everyone by beginning her speech. Lainey's mother, an English PhD, had polished her comments. She read them aloud with ease, a bright smile on her face, and even managed to contain her emotions when mentioning the find had been made in honor of her late brother. *Thanks for the help, little bro.*

As planned, Mitch took his turn at the lectern. He wore a scarlet and grey tie to compliment his dark suit. His portion of the reveal centered on giving credit to The Ohio State University for having the educational programs that had given Lainey, Joan, and himself the proper knowledge to conduct a successful archeological expedition. She gave him an attentive look when he specifically mentioned that he'd be applying for tenure in the geology department.

After the flurry of questions and being asked to pose for an abundance of pictures, she retreated once again into the quiet of the small antechamber off the press room. Mitch joined her and closed the door behind them. "That went extraordinarily well. Thank you again for inviting me to participate."

"I'll do everything I can to help you earn tenure." She leaned in her gaze deep into his eyes.

Lainey barely had the last word out of her mouth when he sealed it with a kiss. His passion unleashed hers. Too bad they were all dressed up and only had moments of privacy. She wanted the kiss to last forever.

In a breathless whisper, she said, "You make me happy."

"I can't wait to see you on campus," was his reply.

* * *

Lainey Shea's Treasure Quest
The Silver Beaver Tokens

Vickey Wollan

Chapter One

With a skittish look over her shoulder, Lainey Shea jerked open the door to the police department. It slammed against the door stop and bounced angrily back at her as she stomped inside. For this time of the afternoon, the place was quiet. She needed the cops to take her seriously about her stalker or she'd get loud, very loud. Inhaling deeply, she told herself to remain calm. It didn't help.

As her eyes adjusted to the fluorescent lighting of the receiving area, Lainey spotted a receptionist behind protective glass. Without waiting for her to look up, she announced, "I'd like to file a stalking complaint."

Startled, the twenty-something woman recovered and leaned toward the circular opening in the window. "Yes, ma'am. Let me call back to see who's available." She punched a few buttons and pushed the microphone of her headset closer to her mouth. "Sir, someone is here with a domestic dispute."

"Nothing domestic about it. I have a stalker," corrected Lainey.

The young lady in an Upper Arlington PD dress shirt gave her a polite grin. "It'll be just a moment if you'd like to have a seat."

Lainey stood her ground, buttoning the jacket of her navy blue power suit. Then she stuffed a tendril of her curly hair back into the tight bun she'd worn to the chamber of commerce luncheon. Being patient while stressed had never been one of her stronger attributes. She crossed her arms over her chest until the door on the opposite side of the tiny box office opened and a distinguished man in uniform poked his head out. "Miss, you caught us at shift change."

Another cop pushed the door all the way open. "I've got it, Sarg. I haven't clocked out yet and am happy to help."

The latest arrival exchanged words with the guy whose shirt showed him to be the commanding officer.

Eventually, the younger guy with tightly cropped dark hair tossed a glance in her direction, his blue eyes bright. "I'll be right with you."

There was something about the enthusiastic officer that she recognized, but the purpose of coming to the police station pushed all other thoughts out of her mind. *You're safe. Hardy can't harass you in here. He can't sink your company.*

Within seconds, the door to her left swung open and the officer, complete with a clipboard, escorted her into a large room with several rows of desks, alive with activity. The walls were covered with protect and serve posters, HR notices, and shift assignment rosters.

"I'll be glad to take your statement, ma'am. I mean miss." He stopped short, and an engaging smile widened across his face. "Wait. I recognize you. Lainey, it's me. Declan. Declan Donnovan. We were neighbors growing up. A bunch of us used to play tag after dinner. You were the fastest runner on the block."

Declan. Wasn't he arrested for grand theft auto? "Sure, I remember. You're a police officer now like your dad." She didn't mean to sound judgmental, but she could hear the edge in her voice. *I can't believe Mr. Bad Boy became a cop.*

A strange volley of emotions rolled across Declan's face so quickly she couldn't discern their meaning. "Dad works for the Columbus PD." He motioned to a door on her right. "Let's use this office for your privacy."

Her four-inch heels clicking on the tile, she followed him to a small, unadorned office that smelled of moldy files. He pulled two chairs to the same side of an empty table so that they faced the window to the main squad room, and she sat in the hard, wooden chair while Declan closed the door and settled in next to her.

His seated posture exuded a masculine authority, yet he relaxed enough to put her at ease. The air-conditioning turned on full blast from the vent behind her. The overly cool air made her tense body shiver.

Putting pen to paper, he asked, "What seems to be the trouble?"

"Ever since I spoke to Bob on the phone, strange things have been happening, and I know Dr. Hardy is behind them." When she played back what she'd just said in her mind, even she realized she sounded a bit disjointed and hysterical.

He'd written, "Bob," then stopped to clarify. "Are you a patient of Dr. Hardy's? Who is Bob?"

"Let me start over. I'm a former student of Mitch Hardy, Ph.D. He's a professor of geology at Ohio State." Lainey, unable to stay in her chair any longer, popped up and paced back and forth.

"I submitted a complaint against him for inappropriate behavior against a student, which kept him from earning tenure. His second attempt, mind you. I put his already downward-spiraling career into a deep freeze. That's why he's coming after me. It's payback."

Declan sat up straighter. "Has he hurt you?"

Lainey swallowed a nervous laugh. The thought of physical harm hadn't occurred to her until just now. "No. He's just trying to scare me, make me miserable."

"In Ohio, you need to file a Civil Stalking Orientated Offense Protection Order against Dr. Hardy. But how does Bob fit into all of this?"

"Hardy hired Bob when we were in Bermuda."

Declan jumped to his feet, his eyebrows pinched together, and a frown formed on his lips. "You went willingly to Bermuda with this man?"

"No." Her shoulders fell as she thought how little this man understood about her situation and how terrified she now was of Dr. Hardy. "This is harder to explain than I expected. The three of us had planned to go out to dinner together, and that's when my roommate, Joan, got sick. Recently, Bob called and admitted that Hardy gave serum of ipecac to Joan. We thought it was a stomach virus."

She collapsed into the closest chair, lowering her head. "Hardy poisoned Joan to get me alone. I fell for it, and I'll never forgive myself." *How could I have let myself be taken advantage of?*

Declan's steel-toed shoes came into view on the scuffed floor. Then his fingers touched hers. She reflexively looked up and batted his hand away.

I can't trust him either. Except for games of tag, where he always made me "it" first, he never gave me the time of day. Only my father hasn't used my compassionate nature against me. All other men are opportunists.

"Look, don't pacify me. Just file the report and help me get a stalking protection order."

He flinched as if he'd touched a hot stove. Then he took a giant sidestep and put his behind in the chair. A new tension took hold of his body as he started to write. "Name – Lainey Shea."

"Helaina. My legal name is Helaina."

Abruptly sliding the clipboard in her direction, his lips pulled into a thin line. "Please fill out the top of the form. We can go through the rest of the questions together."

While Lainey did as he asked, a sound outside the office drew her attention. A group of men had gathered at a nearby desk to stare at her through the glass. Being a Barbie doll in a store display would have generated fewer onlookers. Declan had noticed, too. He gave them an energetic wave of his arm and a stern look. Awkwardness filled each of their stances until they stumbled in all directions, trying to hide their obvious curiosity.

She placed the pen on the form, narrowed her eyes, and clenched her jaw. Men would be off limits in her life for a long time to come. Shaking her head, she moved her chair so she could put her back to the looky-loos.

"Sorry about that. New recruits." As Declan reviewed her answers his expression became animated. "You own a business. Lainey Shea's Treasure Quests."

"I have a Ph.D. in archaeology. People hire me to find valuable artifacts, family heirlooms, or lost treasures." Showing he could be chivalrous didn't make him dating material, even if he did an amazing job of filling out his uniform.

As the wheels of his mind turned, she didn't know if she should interpret the short delay as a compliment or insult. In her current mood, she went with insult. "A woman can manage an expedition as well as any man."

Redness filled his cheeks. "Agreed. That wasn't where ... I mean ... I might have a job for you."

Her fledgling business needed the work. It was her way of keeping Frank's memory alive, and she needed at least one new paying client a month. Her voice dripped with sarcasm, anyway. "You want to hire me?"

"Well, I need to talk it over with my brothers, but yes."

She pinned him with a stare. He didn't blink. "I require a retainer before I start researching a job."

He nodded. "A consummate professional would." His killer smile showed off perfectly straight teeth. "I'm off tomorrow. Can I buy you a cup of coffee?"

Even if she didn't think too highly of her former neighbor, she couldn't turn down a paying client. "You know the bakery on Main and Fifth? Meet me there at nine."

"Done." The smile went away. "Now, tell me more about Hardy. Can you prove he's the one harassing you?"

"Proof?" She tilted her head from one side to the other. "Like what?"

Declan leaned back and straightened his name badge. "Copies of a threatening email or text. A picture of him on your property."

Lainey surveyed the scars in the wood of the old table where she sat and then looked away at the worn filing cabinets. "This loser is smarter than people give him credit for. I go out into the parking lot, and the air has been let out of my tire. A pizza with anchovies gets delivered to my house. I hate anchovies."

Her gaze swiveled back to Officer Donnovan. "Oh, out in the field, someone has been tailing me. One of my clients noticed the glare of binocular lenses and mentioned it. We were in a rural area with no other humans around. I'm not being paranoid. Even the client said it was creepy."

"So, no proof." Declan checked a box on the form. "Can you get Bob to make a formal statement?"

"No one answers the phone number he used to call me. No voicemail, nothing. So, I doubt it." She shrugged and fidgeted with her purse.

"He's playing mind games, but at least he hasn't caused any permanent harm," replied Declan.

When her view swung in his direction, his steely blue eyes showed his concern. Maybe he'd matured from his juvenile delinquent days. Best to keep him at arm's length, anyway. At least she'd completed the task her father had requested. She'd formally told the local police about her concerns. Unfortunately, she didn't feel any safer.

If Declan—and that was a big if—became a paying client, she'd have to go out into the field. Being at her home or office was frightening enough. She'd be more vulnerable in some remote location. The beat of her quickening pulse in her ears drowned out the buzz of the overhead lighting. To make matters worse, she wasn't sure Declan could be trusted. Lainey took in a deep breath and let it out slowly.

* * *

A short time later, Declan closed his locker to be greeted by a trio of rookies who had already changed into their civilian clothes. One of them had gone overboard applying a musky cologne. He tried to take the interruption in stride. The clang of another locker being slammed shut was just another noise to him. Being on the force for six years, he'd been accepted into the family of people on the job. Remembering how hard he'd worked to gain respect; he gave these newbies the benefit of the doubt. "What can I do for you?"

"The looker. She knows you from somewhere, right?" asked the tallest guy with a bit of blond fuzz on his upper lip he probably wished could pass as a mustache.

The brawniest of the trio came forward. "I want dibs on asking her out."

Catching on, Declan tried to let them down easy. "Sorry, guys. She'd never date a cop. Trust me. We went to school together. Cops need a strong woman to be their wife. She's a pampered princess."

"Don't want a bride. I'd like to ride that filly if she'll have me," said the third Musketeer from the back row.

Declan's eyebrows shot up before he could stop them. He didn't want to date Lainey, but he didn't want these hooligans putting their paws on her either. He remembered Lainey being among the people who'd assumed his guilt when he'd been accused of stealing a car. Not to mention her being the academic type like her parents, which also made her out of his league. His opposite at the very least. Except the oath he took to protect and serve included her, even if she needed to be saved from the lusting ambitions of fellow officers.

"Look, I'm meeting her for coffee tomorrow to discuss business. If she's into dating cops, I'll get back to you." Declan gathered up his duffel bag.

"Oh, I see how it is. You want her for yourself. That's all you had to say, man," scoffed the lanky blond.

"You couldn't pay me to date her," replied Declan to the backs of his coworkers as they shuffled away, laughing amongst themselves. Being beautiful doesn't make a woman worth the hassle. At least, he saved himself from the dressing down she'd give him when her date with one of them didn't go well.

* * *

The next morning, Declan softly tapped his thumbs on the small rectangular table to the drum solo playing in his head. Picking a seat by the floor-to-ceiling window at the front of the eating area gave him a good view of the parking lot while he waited for Lainey to arrive. His father had instilled the importance of timeliness into all three sons, including himself, the black sheep middle child. The bell jingled when Lainey opened the door. Five minutes late. He'd try not to hold that against her.

Greeting her in the middle of the room, he couldn't help but notice how her frilly blouse and black slacks showed off her curves. Suddenly feeling underdressed, he tried to flatten a few of the wrinkles in his t-shirt and wished he'd worn his newest pair of jeans. At least he was better dressed than many of the bakery's current patrons. "I'm buying. Please, place your order first."

She seemed less stressed and skittish, but he prepared himself for another anxiety-ridden download, anyway.

With their coffee and muffin purchased, he waved her toward a booth. "My brothers are on board with my idea. Let's see if you think this treasure hunt is viable." He did his best to contain his inner excitement.

"This is a birthday gift for our mother. The woman has everything we can think to buy her, so we're hoping to flush out this story passed down by her great-great-grandfather. At the very least, I want to have a scrapbook and a video that documents everything. Since her multiple sclerosis diagnosis, she's liked being able to live vicariously through her son's outdoor adventures. Maybe all she'll get is a laugh while she turns the pages, but our good intentions will be conveyed." He took a bite of his blueberry confection and tried to gauge if she took his comment seriously.

With a look of compassion, Lainey leaned forward, causing a tendril of her long curls to fall over her shoulder. "I'm sorry to hear about your mom. I didn't know."

"You couldn't have. She was diagnosed after your family moved away." A sweetness filled his nose, and he wasn't sure if it was the pastry or the scent of her shampoo. He gave her a half-hearted grin, trying to bring her back to the subject of treasures.

It must have worked, because her concern turned into a broad smile. "Oral histories passed down through the generations are the best hunts. I found jewels because of the story my three times great-grandfather passed to my father."

"How do you know if it's a big fish tale or a description of real events?"

"I cross reference verifiable facts with archaeological antiquity references and geographical maps. There's still no guarantee." Her smile fell away, and she adopted an all-business posture, as if she'd started a game of chicken, daring him to disagree with her.

"I'm sure you have some sort of contract and guidelines, right?" He mentally gave himself a pep talk. *You're smart. Be firm but polite.*

"Of course. Give me your email, and I'll send you the template right now." She gave him her phone open to a contact entry. It was his turn to fill out the form.

When he returned her cell, he unintentionally looked deep into her brown eyes. Her beauty was too much. He averted his gaze out the window. *Don't do that again. She's your contractor, nothing more. Keep a position of strength in this transaction.*

She tapped her screen several times and put it down. "The client always maintains control of the budget. I don't spend a dime without approval."

The vice grip around his gut relaxed. "Good to know."

"So, tell me the story."

"In 1795, give or take a year, Claude Fontaine trapped beavers for the Hudson's Bay Company in Canada. He and his crew had just gotten paid in solid silver tokens smelted into the shape of a beaver. Fontaine kept the tokens in a leather pouch that hung around his neck. An outlaw attacked just as the sun rose and stole the silver. Claude chased after him to the Canadian border, but the robber had a small rowboat waiting on the shore and made his way to what is now Drummond Island, Michigan."

Declan took a swig of coffee and continued. "Local Indians witnessed the pursuit in progress and let Claude borrow a canoe. Wouldn't you know Fontaine caught up to the guy, but by then he'd dropped off the loot. The thief never confirmed where he'd hidden the silver. To this day, it's never been reported as found as far as we know."

Lainey perked up. "That does sound intriguing. Once you and your brothers sign and transfer the research fee, I can get started."

"You think it's worth looking into?" Declan wanted the story to be real, if only for his mother's sake.

"Well, silver is worth about twenty-four dollars an ounce. Guessing one ounce per token, how many tokens would it take to be worth it to you and your brothers?"

"Proving the truth of the tale may be more valuable than the tokens themselves. Let me get back to you." He continued to finish his breakfast and make idle chit-chat with Lainey. Being around her became more cordial.

With a half-hearted grin and as calm as you please tone, she asked, "The car thing didn't keep you from becoming a cop?"

He didn't see that question coming and couldn't believe she'd asked. "You didn't see the updated social media posts? I was acquitted. I had to do the detective work myself to find the security footage to prove I was across town when that car got jacked."

"Oh. We'd moved away before that. You and I had lost touch. The rumor mill must have gotten the better of me." She stared at her lap while he did his best not to pound his fists on the table.

At least she'd had the decency to act embarrassed. "Your business must be desperate if you're willing to let a reformed criminal hire you."

"We're a start-up, but not desperate." Her nostrils flared as she shot back her reply.

"Right, you've got your parents' money to back you up." The feisty comeback flew out of his mouth before he had a chance to engage his brain.

"Do you want to hire me or not?" Lainey gathered her phone, dropping it in her purse. Then she rose from the bench of the booth and stood over him awaiting his reply.

"It's up to my brothers as much as it's up to me."

"Fine. I'll await your answer, one way or the other. Thanks for breakfast. Enjoy the rest of your day." She rushed across the bakery and out the door with long, determined strides.

It annoyed Declan that the subject of the car theft still got under his skin. Everyone the arresting officer told had easily considered him guilty, including his father and oldest brother. Why wouldn't everyone else? It cut him to the core.

Getting the truth out to reverse those preconceived notions had proven incredibly difficult, and after the accusation, he found himself taking on a bad-boy persona. It just seemed easier. People treated him differently, so he used it to his advantage. *Why can't I be myself, succeed, and find a woman who loves me for the real me?* What was the old saying? Good guys always finish last.

Stuffing the rest of his muffin in his mouth, his tastebuds enjoyed the sugary breakfast. Until he finished the last of his bitter black coffee. Then he realized she'd made a fast exit without touching her food. No way was he letting good grub go to waste. He rewrapped her warm pastry and kept it before cleaning off the table.

If Lainey still believed the lie, it would make keeping the effects of her womanly attractiveness at bay easier. With the truth out, he'd have to rely on another tool. Maybe using his bad boy persona would be his saving grace.

Chapter Two

A few weeks later, just after the Fourth of July, Lainey drove her silver Lexus hybrid, a doctorate graduation gift from her parents, to Declan's house. She'd put a great deal of effort into being early for the launch of this treasure hunt. Her roommate and recent Ph.D. grad, Joan, sat in the passenger seat, rambling on about some historical something. Lainey half-heartedly listened while she rechecked her task list. It pleased her beyond words that Joan had been able to take time off from her day job and had agreed to join the expedition without charging a consulting fee.

She had to admire Declan's negotiating skills. To make the budget work, Lainey agreed to pay for Joan's meals and other expenses out of her so-called profit, though barely breaking even more closely resembled reality. A good review would draw more paying customers, she told herself. Now, she had to find the treasure to earn it.

"Do you think it will be less muggy so close to Canada?" Joan's commentary changed direction.

"I hope so. The humidity makes my hair a frizzy mess." She used her blinker as she did what her GPS told her to do and turned right into an older section of town. Based on the age of the homes and that many were now considered fixer-uppers, she understood how Declan could afford to live in what most considered the affluent town of Upper Arlington, Ohio.

"People would kill for your hair. All long and full of soft curls," replied Joan as she blew out a breath that sent her straight, fine bangs aloft.

"My hair is nothing special."

"Tell yourself that the next time some guy trips over his feet trying to get a better look at you." Joan mimed her way through a demonstration within the confines of her seatbelt.

Lainey let loose with a hearty chuckle. "Thanks. I needed that."

"I figured." Joan gave a wimpy, backhanded smack across Lainey's shoulder. "The start of a hunt always has you on edge."

"This one more than others." She looked both ways before pulling into an intersection.

"Why? Your rigorous due diligence shows this location as highly plausible."

"Because I know Declan and his family. We used to be neighbors." She did her best to smile, but the acid splashing around in her stomach dimmed her enthusiasm.

"I can't wait to lay eyes on this guy. He's got to be beyond hunky. That's what's got you out of sorts, not your hunting skills."

Lainey took a deep breath and did her best to think of a witty comeback—but failed. "He's all right. I'm not interested."

"Uh huh."

Joan had turned away to hide her expression. Lainey recognized her best friend's tactic. "Help me find the house. Two story, red brick."

"There. On the right, three houses up," said Joan.

Lainey eased her new SUV to the curb and put it in park. *Please, let this be a successful hunt.*

A young man in jeans and a t-shirt strolled down the driveway with a wave.

Joan's head swiveled back in Lainey's direction with one eyebrow raised. "He's pretty attractive."

"That's not Declan."

"Darn."

"I'm thinking that's his younger brother, Andre. He's grown up a bit since I last saw him." She waved back.

"The brother that's coming with us?"

A giggle welled up inside her at the hopeful grin on Joan's lips. "Let's go find out."

Exiting the car, she took a moment to allow her business persona to emerge. "Hello. We're with Lainey Shea's Treasure Quest. I'm Lainey."

"I'm Andre. Declan's inside. Let me help you load your gear into my truck."

The double set of dimples, a signature trait of the Donnovan men, made themselves visible. She tried to relax. She needed this brother to be on her side as well. The trio of brothers had pooled their funds together after all.

"I can transfer the equipment. You go find Declan," Joan volunteered. To Andre, she said, "I'm Joan, the historian, we'll be teaming up on this expedition."

Andre seemed duly impressed. Joan nodded at the house and gave Lainey two quick blinks. Lainey took the hint and left her second in command to supervise the details, the thing she did best.

"The sliding glass door in the back is unlocked. Go ahead and let yourself in," added Andre.

As Lainey made her way toward the house, she enjoyed the sun on her face and took in the smell of freshly cut grass. From various conversations used to set up the trip, she understood that this was Declan's house and that he rented rooms to Andre and another officer. The lawn and exterior were immaculate. She tamped down a bit of envy since her parents had cosigned for her condo. He'd done better for himself than she'd expected.

When she peeked inside, she couldn't see anyone. "Hello," she called out as she pulled on the door's latch. "It's Lainey." No answer. Her chest tightened as she entered in slow motion.

The inside of the house didn't match the curb appeal. The scent of sawdust tickled her nose. Except for the renovation debris, the orderly cleanliness of the house surprised her. It wasn't a stereotypical bachelor pad. Most of the interior work seemed well underway, but the original components of the interior showed its age, like the olive and yellow décor in the kitchen from the 1970s. She tiptoed around a stack of old floorboards that must have come from the living room, since half of those planks seemed new. As she walked past a big screen TV, she noticed a doorway on her left.

A shirtless Declan darted toward a chest of drawers, and then, without appearing to see her, he strolled out of sight again.

Should I say something? But the activity in the other room kept her silent. He moved in front of a mirror in the corner and held out two shirts. Having made his decision, he pitched one and yanked the other off its hanger. The muscles in his back and arms rippled. He'd filled out his uniform well, but this view outshined what she'd imagined.

Before she could make a sound, he stuffed his arm into a sleeve, started tucking in the shirttail, and then unzipped his jeans to better finish the task. She did an immediate about-face. It was all she could think to do. *Maybe I can go back outside? He'll never know I was here.*

Putting one speedy step in front of the other, she'd almost made her way back into the kitchen when a cuckoo clock struck ten in the morning. Startled, she gasped. Then she stubbed her toe where the old living room wood sat below the new kitchen tile.

"Ouch!" She slapped a hand over her mouth and caught herself with the other on a counter to keep from sprawling into a complete faceplant. A loud crack—or was it a pop?—filled the air. Then the pain in her toe became her main priority. So much for a stealthy escape. No sense in trying to deny she'd been in his house. Rubbing the top of her injured big toe with the bottom of the other, she stood with her back to the living room and waited for Declan to find her.

"How much of that did you see?" Anger or maybe it was embarrassment dripped from his every word.

"Nothing indecent, I promise. I'm sorry. Andre said to come in. I called out to you. Obviously, not loudly enough." It was hopeless. Each new set of words dug her into a deeper hole. She turned her gaze to the flooring that had been her demise, but not before she caught a glimpse of the redness of Declan's face. The hue of a Santa Claus suit paled in comparison.

"Did you dislodge the tile tripping on it?" He knelt to inspect for damage.

Is he really more concerned about the floor than the well-being of my toe? She took a cleansing breath. "Your craftsmanship is extraordinary."

"Not helping," he snarled.

As he got back on his feet, he gave her a once-over.

Try as she might, she couldn't help but see a wonderful dusting of dark hair across his chest where his shirt hung open. Not too much, but enough to say mature male. Just what she liked. *Oh, how I wish I could unsee that. This is just another treasure hunt, my profession, my way to make a living.*

He quickly buttoned up the rest of his shirt. A crack of leather startled her again as he yanked his belt into place and threaded it through each loop. When he finished dressing, he said, "Look at you. Full hair and makeup like you're going to the mall. We're going to the middle of nowhere. Roughing it. Can you deal with that?"

His anger she could understand. Now, he had the nerve to question her ability to be in the field. That hurt. Since he'd paid a deposit, she took his insult in stride and summoned her professionalism.

"This is a travel day. Tomorrow, we get serious. I've been on digs all over the world. I assure you I'm prepared to be in the wilderness."

She looked him straight in the eye, almost challenging him to underestimate her again. With exceptional focus, she stared into the depths of his soul.

Something in his demeanor changed, and she wasn't sure she liked it.

"Let's start over." His voice was soft and calm. He walked back into the bedroom. A moment later, he returned with his luggage. "I take pride in my work of rehabbing houses. Thank you for noticing. Shall we join the others?" He slid the glass door open and motioned her through.

If he can act like nothing happened, then so can I. The sight of Joan repositioning crates in bed of Andre's double-cab truck with a cap on its bed lifted her spirits. Work she could do. "Let's find some silver beaver tokens for your mother."

* * *

Luckily, during the long car ride to Drummond Island, Michigan, Joan and Andre carried most of the conversation. Declan called shotgun, and Lainey sat behind Andre. Everyone seemed relaxed during the journey, but Declan never looked in her direction. Not once. She guessed she deserved the cold shoulder. As long as he remained a good worker bee under her command, she could deal with any attitude he cared to dish out.

"Let's find a flat spot fairly close to the lake," suggested Lainey.

"Tents should always be placed on higher ground," Declan replied as he motioned for Andre to turn left, away from the water's edge.

She bit her lip and swallowed hard.

Once all the equipment that needed to come out of the truck was on the ground, Lainey opened a topographical map to see how it compared to the reality of their campsite.

"In order: tents, dinner, and if we have time, then you can look at your maps." Declan held out the tent's carrying bag.

"Look, Mister Boy Scout, we have two hours of daylight. I can put up my tent and finish dinner in an hour. The success of this hunt is on me. I'm in charge. Are we good?" She grabbed the tent from him, dropped it, and then returned to her map.

"Yes, ma'am. All good here." Andre hurried up and pulled Declan away by one arm.

Lainey now better understood why her father seemed a bit distant toward her while in the field. Carrying the weight of the mission on one's shoulders wasn't easy. Especially if an exceptionally handsome man wanted to be king of the hill.

* * *

Always an early riser, Declan awoke the next morning before dawn. He snuck out of his tent with his toiletry kit and flashlight and climbed to the highest peak he could find. Fresh morning air wafted past him on a cool breeze, and dew clung to the foliage all around him. He took the moment of solitude to reflect on and process the whispered tongue-lashing his younger brother had given him last night after they were all in their tents.

"Take it down a notch, bro," Andre had said. "I can't make the video for mom if you're constantly arguing with Lainey. We hired her. Now let her do her job."

The purpose of this whole trip was to give his mother something to make her happy. Even if it was a video of Andre and him making fools of themselves while digging for a treasure that may not exist.

When the first golden beam of sunlight graced the sky, he positioned his tiny mirror in the crux of a tree branch facing east and used his battery-operated razor to remove the stubble from his face. His freshly groomed reflection showed the disappointment he had in himself. *Be the dutiful cop on the street and follow the chain of command.* He took a deep breath and counted to ten.

The snap of a broken twig behind him put him on high alert. Bracing for combat, he called out, "Andre, is that you?"

"It's Lainey. Mind if I join you?" She hopped over some weeds and closed the gap between them.

She'd pulled her curly locks into some sort of braid that revealed more of her creamy complexion. Growing hues of yellow and orange framed her silhouette, the rounding of her hips and narrow waist as visible as ever in her cargo shorts and tucked in t-shirt.

She lowered the lantern she carried to her feet, then raised it to her head. "Look. Cloddy hiking boots and no makeup."

The dim light had no chance of hiding her exquisite features. His stomach flipped when her long eyelashes fluttered. Not fair.

"Making my mom happy is important to me. I was out of line yesterday." That was as close to an apology as he could muster.

"Since you're an early bird like me, we'll get along just fine." She gave him an energy bar and turned to survey the land before them.

"What's the plan?" He opened the wrapper and took a bite.

Holding up the lantern once more, she swung it left and then right. "I want to find the biggest erosion gully caused by ice melt runoff and follow it. Not enough sunlight yet."

Lainey hung the lantern on a nearby branch and opened a bar for herself. He stood with her in silence as he finished his organic oats and maple breakfast. The higher the sun rose in the sky, the lower his anxiety fell into his subconscious, but his urge to hold her in his arms remained the same.

* * *

Several hours later, Declan stopped for another handful of trail mix. He hadn't been that physically active, but his stomach growled as if he'd run a marathon. Although surrounded by heavy brush, this small field of wildflowers was a great place for a break.

Earlier, before he'd left camp, Andre had videoed him and the ladies as they looked at maps and pounded markers into the ground. He'd been able to give his mother a genuine, wide smile and heartfelt wave into the camera lens. Now, the tedious task of plotting possible dig sights had him questioning if the treasure ever existed. Not that he expected to find silver in an hour or two, but the fact that Lainey had assigned Joan and Andre tasks in the opposite direction, leaving him to deal with her most of the morning, didn't help. If it had been under different circumstances, he'd applaud the way she took charge. Taking orders from Miss Beyond Attractive, though, continued to be a challenge.

A low grunt made the hairs on the back of his neck stand on end. The fact its direction put Lainey much closer to it than himself had alarm bells going off.

"Lainey, come to me. Now. I mean, right now." His heart rate doubled.

Without running, she quickly bounded to his side. At least he could trust her to do as she was told when it mattered.

"Did you hear that?" He put himself between her and the danger.

"Yep. Sounds big." She grabbed his forearm. "Coyotes, I can handle. Bears, not so much."

Then, a medium-sized black bear rushed at them from the tree line. When the bear laid eyes on two humans, he launched himself to his full height and let loose a toothy snarl.

"Rawr!" Lainey shouted in the direction of the bear, flailed her arms, and jumped around.

She responded correctly when encountering a bear. He was impressed.

Declan threw his backpack on the ground and retrieved his service firearm, tucking the cold, hard metal into the front of his belted shorts, just in case. "Git! Go! Shoo!" He clapped his hands with great speed and force.

The bear lowered to all fours but let loose another terrifying roar. Its nostrils flared.

"He smells something. I don't have any food on me. Do you—" Lainey cut off her question and glared at him. "The trail mix. Give him your trail mix."

With a hesitant gait, he shuffled to his bag. She was right. Why didn't he think of that? It knocked his survivalist pride down a notch.

Yanking the zipper on the pocket of his sack, Declan hauled out the plastic bag and threw the fastest fast pitch he'd ever thrown in his life. The dried raisins, cranberries, and banana chips landed well past the bear, back towards the bushes from which it had emerged.

The bear grunted and heaved his head from side to side, but eventually turned tail and hastened his exit, engulfing the Ziplock into his huge jaws as he darted back into the underbrush.

"That was close." Declan tried to slow his breathing as he put his nine-millimeter into its holster and stowed it in his backpack.

"I have more trail mix back at base camp."

He nearly gotten her by mauled a bear, and she was worried about his lost food. He scratched his head. "My appetite just died."

When Lainey trotted along the line of prints left by the bear, Declan threw his hands in the air and bellowed, "What are you doing?"

"We need to make sure he's gone." She said it with such a matter-of-fact tone, it made his mind spin.

Within seconds, his trusty sidearm was back in his right hand as he tossed his backpack over his shoulder with his left. "Let me lead. I'm armed."

"Fine."

Does this woman have a death wish?

Thinking he'd traveled far enough without seeing the bear, he stopped.

Lainey pushed past him, her gaze still fixed on the impressions left by the bear's paws.

"What? Are you a tracker, too?"

Her face flashed in his direction and then whipped forward again. "Yes, actually."

"Really? I was kind of kidding."

"Look." She pointed at the grass pressed into the mud. "An empty sardine can. The lid's right over there."

She picked it up and stuck her nose in it.

At the thought of smelling sardines, his stomach turned sour.

"This is fresh. Recently opened." With elongated strides, she marched down the path. "Seriously? There's another one."

Now, he was hot on her heels. "There are two more up ahead."

Like Hansel and Gretel, he and Lainey followed the trail of cans that had clearly been left on purpose.

"Why would someone lead a bear to our location?" Declan turned toward Lainey who had gone completely pale. He reached for her.

She shook uncontrollably. "Hardy! He's stalking me. Wants to hurt me. Now do you believe me?"

"Yes. Always have."

With slow movements, he maneuvered to face her and pulled her to his chest, encircling her within his arms. The tremble that jolted through her body was obvious. It broke his heart. The woman could stare down a bear, but this professor guy could unnerve her. This trip now had two missions. Make Mom happy and bring Dr. Hardy to justice

Chapter Three

The following morning, Lainey called an impromptu meeting around Andre's vehicle. "Let's all carry bear spray today and lock up the remaining food in the truck's backseat."

She expected pushback from Declan. Surprisingly, he simply nodded. Over dinner the previous night—canned beef stew warmed on a metal grate over the fire—Declan re-enacted Lainey's thrashing arm movements used to scare the bear. She laughed along with everyone else but had hoped he'd give her credit for not panicking or making the situation worse. *Some men can't allow a woman to lead.*

When she unfurled the map and pointed at where she wanted to dig around the lake's edge, Declan undermined her authority. Again.

"You three can have a good time standing in sludge." He pointed due north. "I'm going to where the biggest ice cave is known to have formed closest to the Canadian Border. The robber definitely hid the loot soon after reaching the shore of this island."

She noticed Joan and Andre's body language. They didn't seem enthused with Declan's plan either. While she took a moment to choose her words carefully, Joan jumped in.

"Bad idea. The beaver tokens have lain on the ground for more than two hundred years. Do you understand how much soil rushing water displaces during that span of time?"

Leave it to Joan to get to the heart of the matter. Andre looked away, a smirk stealthily hidden from his brother's view.

"Due to safety concerns, we'll stick together, or I can call off this hunt and give you a full refund," Lainey said, her face proactively pulled into a scowl.

"To the water we go." Declan's words said agreement, but his tone dripped with sarcasm.

No matter. She was in charge.

After about fifteen minutes of brisk hiking, leading the group while making her own path through tall weeds, Lainey reached the shoreline. If they had camped by the lake as she'd asked, there would have been more time to dig. Yesterday's decision could not be easily changed, so she retrieved her trusty compass and surveyed the portion of the small body of water closest to Canada. "Joan, do you see the white pine that's fallen into the water? You take Andre and start with the metal detector there. The plan is to meet back here for lunch."

It pleased her to witness Andre following Joan and accepting her instructions without hesitation.

Now to contend with the naysayer. "We're going to go in the opposite direction. I have a hunch the most likely place to find the treasure is where the small trickles build into a sizable stream, which connects about forty meters east of here."

Declan dutifully picked up the heaviest gear and waved for her to lead. "I still think this is the wrong location."

"Forget that I've been studying archaeology for eight years. I've also been on digs with my father for as long as I can remember. He'd pick this spot, too, because I'm following his scouting method."

He didn't unleash a snarky comeback. Maybe he respected her father, and she only needed to prove herself?

Several nearby streams fed the small lake, but only one came from due north. Since it was summer, the speed of the water was nothing more than a slow trickle to a medium flow. The moist creek bed gave way to short grass, tall weeds, then pine trees of varying heights with a great number of shrubs and vines tangled in between. Breaks in the foliage came from rocky overhangs and boulders of all sizes. An untouched wilderness for certain.

She coached him on how best to use the digging tools and sent him farther upstream. Comfortably alone under the headset of her equipment, Lainey found her happy place. Her heart skipped a beat with each beep of her detector. She'd found nothing noteworthy, but the effort soothed her anxiety. Every ten minutes or so, she scanned in a full circle to confirm the wildlife and Professor Hardy weren't in her vicinity. The rhythm of her routine numbed her senses.

Something briskly brushed her arm, and she nearly screamed. Yanking off her headset, she glared at Declan.

"Sorry, I need a break. I figured you did, too." He held out a bottle of water. "Dynamite could have gone off next to you, and I'm not sure you would've reacted. We're still in bear country."

He had a point, and his expression showed concern. "Thanks. I often scan for wildlife while I'm listening for the beeps."

She sat on a big boulder, and he joined her. The sun's height in the sky told her it was mid-morning. Heat came at her on the humid breeze. She did her best to retighten her ponytail as tendrils of frizzy curls fell in her face. A few birds chirped. Her enjoyment of the sounds of nature, however, was interrupted when he asked, "Can I get something off my chest?"

Like I have a choice. "Sure." She took a long gulp of cool water.

"I'm jealous of you."

Her eyebrows rose a bit as her mouth fell open.

"You have this wonderful relationship with your dad. I envy that."

"Our relationship isn't always perfect," she replied.

"Did he accuse you of grand theft auto without hearing your side of the story?"

"No."

The slouch of his shoulder and the pain on his face gave her pause.

"I'm rough around the edges, I know. I have my reasons. Please, know that I'm a better person than anyone gives me credit for being." With his statement of truth made, he hopped off the rock and headed back to where he'd been working without looking back.

Where did that come from? Her concern about her inability to judge men cracked a bit. Just because Hardy was a jerk didn't mean all men were. She'd have to ask Joan. She trusted Joan's judgement about men much better than her own. Maybe Declan could be taken off the naughty list. He'd done a wonderful job of saving her from the bear, and that hug after her mentioning Hardy had been just what she needed.

She picked up her detector again, and time passed. Her gaze studied the widest portion of the stream's silt brought from higher altitudes during the annual spring thaw.

A flash of light made her look up.

Before she could react, Declan tackled her, pushing her backwards. She lost her footing, and her behind landed in the stream with a splash. The force of his contact nearly jarred her headset off. Reaching up to her ears, she did her best to keep it from getting wet.

His hardened face was inches from hers. "Stay down. Danger."

She became a statue as frigid moisture crawled up her back and down her thighs. "Where?"

"A laser beam pointed at your chest." He pushed up and turned to look back over his shoulder.

A shot rang out.

She expected to feel pain. He threw himself on her. Then, she feared for his safety. He'd used his body to cover hers.

"Are you hit?"

"No. You?"

"No."

"I don't think the gunner meant to shoot us. The bullet ricocheted off a tree over our heads. If he wanted to hurt us, he wouldn't have aimed so high." Declan lifted off her once more and army-crawled, staying low, searching in the direction where the gunfire had originated.

Remaining laid out on the ground, she rolled out of the water. Smoke from the fired round filled her nose. "Do you see him?"

"Listen. If he's running, we might be able to hear his location," whispered Declan.

She held her breath and put all her energy into the use of her ears.

The swish of tall grass and the snap of a branch breaking told her the shooter fled toward the north—the direction of their camp.

"Declan!" The anguished sound of Andre's scream amplified her fear.

"We're good. Stay where you are."

How could Declan be so calm? His fingers wrapped around her wrists as he hauled her to her feet.

"Leave everything and run," ordered Declan.

She stayed with him as he raced along the tree line, darting from one piece of cover to another. A large rock, then to the next wide trunk. No additional cracks of gunfire startled her, but she couldn't pinpoint the shooter's location.

When they ducked behind a huge rock, she asked, "Do you think he's gone?"

"For now."

He gave her an obvious, slow look from head to toe.

She wanted to be insulted until she realized his concern was for her wellbeing. "I'm wet and dirty but fine." Looking him over, she noticed a trickle of blood on his forearm. Something must have scratched him when he tackled her. She reached to touch it, and he scowled.

"Leave it be. I'm fine." With a quick flick of his head, he looked out past the rock in Andre's direction. "Clear. Grab your gear and come back."

"Roger that," shouted Andre.

I'm among a family of cops. What a great choice in clients to have about now. She leaned back against the rock and did her best to stop gasping for air.

"Stay here. I'm going back for the equipment." Declan said.

"Don't be a hero and chase after him alone."

He gave her the strangest look and jogged away.

Just as Andre and Joan found her by the water's edge, Declan returned with the metal detector and the cooler on his shoulders. His backpack was in one hand and his gun in the other.

"What was that? Some stupid hunter?" Andre reached out to lighten Declan's load. "Only problem is, nothing is in season right now."

"I imagine this was another attempt by Dr. Hardy to scare Lainey out of business and ruin her career. Pure revenge." Joan gave her a big hug. Then pulled back with a start. "You're wet."

"Better wet than shot." She looked in Declan's direction. "Thank you, for yesterday and today."

Declan gave her a single nod and one of his dimpled smiles. "I vote for an early lunch so Lainey and I can change into some dry clothes."

How he could smile after being shot at, she couldn't fathom.

Andre said, "We need to devise a security detail alongside a treasure-hunting detail."

"On that, we can agree." Declan put an arm around her shoulder and pulled her close.

Lainey let him. She wasn't sure if she could allow romance into her life, but she could let him protect her. He seemed to have a knack for it.

* * *

About an hour later, the throb in Declan's head finally subsided when the local deputy's squad car pulled up to the campsite. Out of an abundance of caution, he'd asked Lainey and Joan to take cover inside their tent. With Lainey out of sight, he could concentrate on giving the deputy as much information as possible.

He'd put his badge on a lanyard around his neck and asked Andre to do the same. He and Andre were both armed now, too. His brother had retrieved his hunting rifle from under the backseat of his truck, and Declan had his service weapon holstered on his belt. No point in having the deputies confuse him or his brother for the suspect.

"Hello, officer." Declan kept his hands up and visible as he approached the cruiser.

The officer exited the car and gave him a slight wave.

Declan continued. "Thanks for coming. I know this is out of your normal patrol area." He lifted his badge, adding, "Off-duty officer, Upper Arlington PD in Ohio."

"What's this about some perp shooting at you?" The deputy pulled a tablet from the passenger seat and prepared to file a report.

"Not attempted murder. More like premeditated harassment." Declan looked at the tent to make certain the ladies remained inside. "Helaina Shea is with us and has a stalking protection order against Dr. Mitch Hardy. I'm assuming either Hardy or someone he hired aimed a rifle laser at her chest. I witnessed it and intervened. The shooter fired a warning shot about ten feet over our heads."

"Did you find a shell casing? Do you know the caliber?" The officer pecked with his index finger on the screen."

"No. But I can take you to the scene, and we can look together." Declan motioned for Andre to join the conversation. "I'll have my brother, who's on the job with Columbus, Ohio PD, stay back to guard the ladies."

"So, no injuries and only one shot fired." The deputy typed, scrolled, and typed some more. "Our department is stretched thin. Could you take photographs? I'll add them to my report."

He clicked the release on his trunk, brought back a small plastic bag with official markings, and gave it to Declan. "You know what to do with this if you find the casing."

"Sure. Thanks for taking our situation seriously." Declan gave the officer a warm smile.

"Of course. We take care of our own." With a nod, he ambled toward the open driver's seat door. "I've got another citizen waiting. Gotta go."

Declan's heart still pumped a bit faster than normal. Having the local law in the loop didn't ease his concern like he'd hoped it would.

"Lainey can wear my spare Kevlar vest," Andre offered. "It's in the back of my truck."

"My gut tells me this Hardy guy doesn't want to hurt her, just wants to ruin her. Let's not make her any more afraid."

"Business as usual?" asked Andre.

"Let's stick together and take more video footage for Mom in that area. I can peel away and look around." A feeling of calm came over Declan. He had a plan. All that went out the window when Lainey's voice wafted his way.

"I'm the tracker, remember? I'll look with you." The flap on her tent unzipped and her head with those glorious curls popped out.

"Were you eavesdropping?" Declan asked.

"It's not like we're in a soundproof booth over here," she grumbled, then crawled out of the tent with Joan right behind her. They both wore fishing wader pants that came well above the waist, hanging off their shoulders with suspenders.

Andre gave him a curious look. "I didn't pack my fishing gear."

"Not going fishing. We're going silver hunting," Joan replied with a giggle.

"Um ... am I missing something? You still want to look?" Declan's headache came back with a vengeance.

Lainey waddled up to him in her ridiculous looking outfit. "You're right. He wants to scare me. Well, I'm not going to let him."

Declan raised an eyebrow, his gaze drifting from Lainey to Joan, then Andre and back to Lainey. Everyone around him seemed to be on the same page. "Let's go then."

While waiting for the deputy to arrive, he'd grabbed a peanut butter and jelly sandwich along with everyone else, so once Lainey told him what equipment bags she wanted, he refocused his energy into being her bodyguard. As it related to security, Lainey began acquiescing to his suggestions. If she continued to acknowledge his law enforcement expertise, in the future, he'd leave the treasure-hunting decisions to her. Maybe once the ground rules were laid, he could work with her. Seriously, he had to give her props for tamping down her fears. The woman had grit. It made him like her more.

Except that was a problem. He'd never dated anyone with a Ph.D. She hadn't lorded her education over him, but what would people think of a cop dating an academic type? It wasn't like his salary compared to her parents or what she'd be making after her business took off, which he was sure it would. Her will and determination almost guaranteed that. *It's no good. Get the woman out of your head. Spare yourself the heartache.*

He had to keep Lainey safe to be able to provide a bit of joy for his ailing mother. With a new focus in the forefront of his mind, he took the lead on the hike back to the lake. A path had begun to form since they'd taken the same route several times. Then Declan remembered Lainey had asked to camp closer to the lake. He gave himself a metaphorical thump on the head and rolled his eyes. Being in front of everyone had its advantages.

When the ladies waded into the lake, Declan shook his head. He didn't understand the need.

"What are they doing?" asked Andre.

"Beats me. I'm going to stand guard until Lainey changes my orders," replied Declan.

Andre turned his rifle away from the water's edge, shaded his eyes with his forearm, and scanned the area, but Declan could still see part of a smirk on his brother's face.

Having his little brother mock him got under his skin. "What?"

"You got it bad for her."

"Do not." Heat rose in his cheeks.

"Keep telling yourself that."

"She's not my type." Declan assumed that would be the last word.

"Your track record with your so-called type is sad. Maybe you need a new type."

Declan choked. Who was his younger brother to give him advice on women? "Keep your eyes peeled."

"Yes, sir."

A splash behind him had him turning toward the water in a hurry. Had she fallen? Did she need his help? *I do care about her. There's no denying it.*

Lainey carried one side of a pole, and Joan worked to keep it level on the other end.

"I took a core soil sample. It'll have to dry before it's any good to us. Yesterday, I took one up on the hill near where you shaved for comparison."

Declan decided to add this to the list of things he didn't understand about her or her strategies. "Sounds good." He hoped that was an appropriate response.

Lainey asked, "Can I try to track the shooter?"

Being her detective and protector, he could manage. "Let me show you the damage on the tree."

Leaving Andre to work with Joan on the science stuff, he led her upstream a few yards. "If we're onto something, maybe Hardy wants to steal it and any publicity about it."

She pulled up short. "You know about that?"

"I googled you and then Hardy. You found the jewels, and for some reason he participated in the press conference." Declan noted her reaction the way he would if she were a suspect.

"He aided in my search. With his tenure on the line, I thought I'd do him a favor. Boy, was I naive. To this day, I don't trust my judgment concerning men." Her expression softened and shifted to sadness.

"Sorry if I touched a nerve. I'm trying to wrap my head around all the possible motives for his actions." He indicated the bark missing from a broad tree trunk and nonchalantly added, "You can trust me."

She didn't say a word. Moreover, she acted like he hadn't said a thing. It cut him deep. *How can I make her believe in me?*

Putting his detective hat on, he put his back to the tree and contemplated the bullet's most likely trajectory. She did the same, allowing her arm to hang beside his. He leaned in her direction until their arms brushed. A divine warmth grew where he touched her.

"I see some trampled grass. Let's check it out." She darted across the stream, her rubber-covered feet making large splashes.

He kept up with her, stepping exactly where she did. His jaw went slack when she pulled herself up the side of a six-foot, rocky cliff face. The heavy waders didn't slow her one bit. She climbed like a mountain goat. It excited him.

Once atop the ridge, she pointed. "Do you see it? Take a picture before we get any closer."

He did as she asked. When she stilled, he rounded a grouping of low shrubs and a young tree, then circled back toward the tall blades of bent grass. It looked like someone had been lying in the weeds. A dank mustiness released from the moist soil with his every step as he took more photos.

"The spent casing would fly to the right, wouldn't it?" she asked.

She was even more beautiful when using her brain. It was almost as if he could see the calculations dance across her features. "You understand guns?"

"I do."

I could love this woman. It took him a split second to gather himself, then he examined the right side of the indentation, where the shooter's s rib cage would have been. Sure enough. The brass of a spent shell teetered in between a couple of weeds. The evidence bag in hand, he pushed the grass, and the remains of the bullet fell inside bag without him having to touch it.

"I got it." He strolled back to her side. "Maybe you should be a private eye instead of a treasure hunter."

She smiled at him. "Both jobs use some of the same skills."

"We should work together more often." He couldn't believe the words slipped from his lips.

She didn't immediately shut down the idea. It gave him hope.

Chapter Four

Shortly before supper that same day, Lainey suggested they all go to a nearby public campground to get cleaned up. She still had mud streaks on her arms from where Declan had tackled her into the stream, and having donned the wader boots, she was sweaty all over. The shower wasn't much more than a trickle, and the water could barely be described as warm, but being clean made her feel so much better. The other benefit was that, with many more people nearby, Hardy wouldn't try anything. At least, that's what she told herself. To save time, she let her hair dry in the summer's hot, evening breeze. Her curls were out of control, anyway. She elected to let them be free.

Luckily, she'd stuffed some extra clothes in her suitcase, figuring she'd need more than one outfit per day. Tonight's ensemble was the least appropriate for field work, so she prepared herself for a snarky comment from Declan about being too girly to rough it. When she joined him after the shower, his comment surprised her.

"That color suits you." Declan chuckled as he put his dirty clothes into a garbage bag and jammed it into his duffel. "If it's Buckeye scarlet, I might have to protect you against the local Michigan Wolverine fans."

Pleased and feeling a bit mischievous, Lainey decided to test his hypothesis. "O-H!" she shouted as loudly as she could.

Somewhere off in the distance, a deep voice replied with, "I-O."

Then another voice chimed in. "Go Blue."

"If that's as rowdy as it gets, I think I'm safe, but thanks for the offer to save me." She gave Declan a gentle punch in the arm.

He frowned dramatically. "Do you always live this dangerously? People up here take their college sports seriously."

It gave her pleasure to get Declan's ire up. "Relax. If it were the day of the Ohio State versus Michigan football game, I'd be more cautious." She laughed. Every part of her enjoyed this moment. Something about showering had temporarily washed away all her concerns.

She filled her lungs with the fresh, city-free air. Being in the outdoors had all kinds of beauty if you allowed yourself to see it. The call of a bird flying overhead made her look up, and she pointed. "Wow, those yellow feathers are so bright."

"That's an American Goldfinch," he said.

She peered at him, a bit surprised. "You know birds?"

"Some. It's kind of a hobby." Declan looked away and back before whispering, "Andre's getting us on camera. Let's talk treasure. Tell me the significance of the soil samples."

She caught Andre's location in her peripheral vision and tried to talk in a natural voice. "The treasure was reportedly hidden in one of the ice caves known to have formed on Drummond Island. The spring thaw causes strong currents that erodes dirt and washes away even heavier items like, say, small silver tokens." She then looked straight into the phone's lens. "I'm trying to determine how far down we'll need to dig."

Joan exited the showers, and Andre clicked off the camera.

"Let's eat. I'm starving," Joan said.

Leave it to her friend to state the obvious.

When they returned to the campsite, Declan asked her to use her tracking skills to see if anyone had messed with anything while they were gone. Her apprehension about being a sitting duck in the middle of nowhere returned. It was the men's turn to cook tonight's gourmet meal of all-beef hotdogs and BBQ potato chips, so she grabbed Joan's arm and towed her to the outer perimeter.

"Look for a big footprint that isn't Andre's or Declan's. They've both been wearing gym shoes," she explained.

Lainey kept her gaze on the ground even as Joan commented, "Kind of nice having a strong, goodlooking guy like Declan as a bodyguard, right?"

"I suppose." She didn't want to go there.

"Andre's great. Being partnered with him is okay by me." Joan's words had a whimsical, singsong lilt to it.

Lainey didn't take the bait. "That's nice." She kept looking and headed east, away from the tents. It wasn't a marked path but a big clearing that could be easily walked. She had traveled far enough away that speaking at a normal volume wouldn't be deciphered by the guys at the campfire, but if she screamed, her clients-bodyguards could still hear her.

Having to think in such terms ratcheted up her unease. The thought that had been swimming in her mind for months finally tumbled out in words.

"I can't believe I let Hardy take advantage of me. I misjudged him so badly."

Joan grabbed her shoulder and turned her around. "I owe you an apology."

"What on earth for?" Lainey looked deep into Joan's eyes. She wasn't sure if they were filled with sorrow or remorse.

Joan wrapped her arms around herself and glanced down. "I had an uneasy feeling about the professor from the first moment I met him. I shouldn't have encouraged you to have dinner with him on Spring Break. This is all my fault."

Lainey pulled her dearest friend into a big hug. "This is Hardy's fault. You did nothing wrong. Don't hold onto any guilt."

"Easy for you to say." Joan pulled out of the embrace, gave her a half-hearted nod, and hiked farther east.

Following behind, over the rhythmic clicks of the crickets, Lainey said, "I've sworn off romance for a long while. I don't trust myself to be a good judge of men. Take Declan for example. He could be a serial killer, and I wouldn't be the wiser."

"Be serious." Joan halted, and Lainey stumbled into her. "Declan has that car thief thing haunting him, but he's a good guy."

"Are you sure?" Lainey tried to ignore the glimmer of hope that welled up inside her.

Joan put her face directly in front of Lainey's. "As much as I had inner alarm bells about Hardy, I have the total opposite feeling about Declan. If I could see auras, his would be the purest."

"If you say so."

"I do." Joan's stomach growled. Let's finish this so I can eat."

Lainey burst out laughing. Joan always had a way to make her feel better. "Let's go another ten feet or so and then go back."

She trudged a few feet forward and stopped on a dime. Her chest tightened while her knees started to knock. A large boot print pointed toward the camp. The indent in the soil had a solid heel and a pointed toe. A cowboy boot. Did Hardy wear boots? She'd never seen any on him. Her view darted right, then left. A tremor ran down her spine. The tracks led into the bushes. This guy had hoped to hide his tracks and could be surveilling her now.

Lainey whispered, "This footprint is fresh. I don't like it. Let's tell the guys. Someone has scouted out our campsite."

With Joan running ahead of her, she raced back to the fire. Her footfalls made loud thuds. Branches cracked under her hurrying feet. Needing to be near Declan, by the man that made her feel safe, she sprinted directly to his side.

"What's wrong?" asked Declan.

"I found tracks. Not ours." Rambling, she spewed the details and her estimation of what they might mean to Declan and Andre.

After hearing what she'd found, the men set up four torches to provide more light around the tents.

"We'll make certain the campfire stays illuminated all night. I don't think this guy wants to be seen, but to be safe, no one goes anywhere alone. We'll take a closer look in the morning."

Declan's deep, commanding voice took the edge off her fears, but only by a small sliver. While eating supper, she put on a brave face, but her muscles grew tight, and her nerves began to twitch. Pulling deep into her thoughts, she revisited what Joan had said. She might not be a good judge of his character; Joan, however, seemed to think highly of Declan. Yes, he was a client, and she had her rules. Business and romance didn't mix. Maybe she could use this trip to see what might be possible after her business with him had concluded.

Lainey's need to release or somehow use up her nervous energy got the better of her. *How the heck am I going to be able to sleep?* Gathering ingredients for a s'more, she sat by the campfire's edge. She dug into the nearby bag of marshmallows and put some extras on her plate. Andre and Joan were deep in conversation and already held skewers over the fire.

Needing a distraction, she picked a target. With a great deal of velocity, she beaned Declan in the chest with a marshmallow. Did he have a playful side, or was he all cop regulations and refurbishing protocols? His head popped up with a curious expression. Then the gleam of his white teeth became evident by the light of the fire.

"You did that on purpose," he accused, his lips curving up.

"What if I did?" She stiffened her back, trying to look indignant.

With a light touch, he propelled one back at her in a high arc. She leaned forward and caught it in her mouth.

"Bravo." He stood to give her an ovation.

She, in turn, thwacked him in the chest again, letting loose a cackle she couldn't contain.

He raised his brows in mock disbelief. "Hey, what did I do?"

Her third volley hit his forehead, neatly bouncing off. He reached out to catch the marshmallow, bobbled it, and eventually caught it, popping it in his mouth. Then winding up like a pitcher, his next attempt grazed her hair as she ducked.

Jumping to her feet, her next lob was off target. He bent low and kept it from landing in the dirt. Firing the soft treat back at her, he ran in her direction. With a half-giggle, half-squeal, she sprinted to her tent. He caught her around the waist, and before she could react, he scooped her up and threw her over his shoulder.

His strength and agility impressed her. She laughed uncontrollably, a marvelous release of stress, and a tiny bit of her began to trust him. "Am I under arrest?"

"Do you need to be?" He marched back to the fire.

She wanted to smack him, except the closest thing within reach at the moment was his derriere. So, she refrained. As he put her back on her feet, she slid down his chest and caught whiff of his woodsy shampoo. Why did he have to smell so good? So male? She tilted up her face just as her mouth passed his. Temptation erupted.

Then Andre's deep voice overpowered the subtle sounds of the night. "I think these two have it bad for each other."

"Agreed," replied Joan with a sigh.

A last little bit of a giggle escaped as she leaned toward Declan's ear to whisper. "I'm glad you have a playful side."

"Of course. But I'll still protect you tomorrow and whenever you need."

On that sobering note, she excused herself to retire in her tent. Her intuition told her the silver beaver tokens were near the stream or lake. She just needed to find them.

* * *

Hearing the tires of a vehicle pulling off the road over the berm's gravel, Declan called out after Lainey. "Hey, the night's young, and it sounds like we're about to have a visitor."

Lainey returned the campfire.

He turned his flashlight toward the sound and relaxed when a sheriff's cruiser came into view. Leaving his low beams on and the door open, the deputy who'd swung by earlier got out.

With a wave he approached the fire. "Evening all. I'm pulling a double shift, so I'm going to patrol this area several times overnight."

Declan scrounged in Andre's toolbox to find the plastic evidence bag. "Here's the shell casing we found. I know it's not enough for an arrest, but at least it's another piece of the puzzle."

The cop tossed the bag onto the driver's seat of his car.

"Are there passable dirt roads between here and the island's edge?" Lainey came to stand beside him. "I spotted a pair of boot prints that don't belong to any of us. They turned into the bushes coming from the east just outside our camp."

"There are." The deputy pulled out his tablet once again. "So, you think the alleged shooter has had eyes on your base camp?"

"I think he's holed up in a tent out of earshot." Lainey pointed at the gap in the trees where she'd found the prints.

"Do you have proof of that?"

"No." Lainey crossed her arms over her chest. "Just a hunch."

Nodding, the officer updated his report.

"Having extra patrols certainly puts my mind at ease. Thanks." Andre joined the conversation.

Joan left the firepit to complete the cluster around the patrol car.

"Don't be alarmed if you hear a car door or me talking on the radio with dispatch. It's pretty remote out here and sound carries. But not many visitors spend the night, so there shouldn't be any other traffic." With a swift salute, the officer got back in his vehicle and backed away from Declan's position.

"Looks like we can be off duty, bro. Let's go make some more s'mores." Andre returned to the trunk of a fallen tree that had been repurposed as a bench. Joan sat beside him, gathering chocolate and graham crackers.

With a flashlight, Declan grasped Lainey's arm. "Since we have added security, why don't we enjoy the stars? The sky is clear. Great view." Declan held his breath, then his heart sank when she walked away.

"Let me get a citronella candle to bring with us." She scratched her thigh. "Stars beautiful. Bug bites bad."

She said yes. She's willing to be alone with me. Maybe I have a shot after all.

Declan led her to the place he'd found for his morning shave—the highest hilltop for miles. There were no other signs of human life as far as he could see. This also seemed to be the rockiest place on the island. He climbed a sizable boulder and pulled Lainey up to join him. As the wind shifted, the fragrant smell of honeysuckle came to his nose. Then he turned his flashlight off and waited for his eyes to adjust.

First, he tried to spot Sirius, the brightest star in the July sky. Then he looked for the summer triangle made from Vega, Deneb, and Altair.

Before he could put his thoughts into words, Lainey commented, "Gee, look at all those satellites. It's easy to mistake a manmade object for a star."

Of course, she'd learned about constellations. Add them to the list. Her brain had to be full of all kinds of information to be an archaeologist. She'd agreed to join him, so he did his best to feel at ease. Her beauty was only outshined by her intelligence. Was that such a bad thing?

"Can I ask you a question? You don't have to answer." Her face tilted in his direction. The deep brown of her eyes was visible in the brightness of the moon.

"Shoot," he replied.

She stiffened.

"Too soon?" His attempt at humor fell flat, so he put on a fake grin. "Ask away." Still over-smiling, he gazed at her while she gathered her words.

"Has your relationship with your dad recovered from the car theft, false accusation thing? The reason I ask is because my dad and I were sideways after the death of my brother. It took a great deal of time and several difficult conversations, but we're good now."

"Dealing with your brother's accident must have been brutal. Sorry." He couldn't fathom how he'd cope with that kind of loss. "To answer your question. No. We Donnovan men don't *talk* well."

"Put the words aside. How does he treat you?"

He had to think about that. "We're civil. I know he loves me, but we're not close. He's always enjoyed hanging out with my brothers more than me."

"I haven't been around your family lately to know." She peered up at the sky. He kept his gaze on her. When she pointed at a shooting star, he noticed goosebumps on her arm and instantly drew her closer to provide warmth. She didn't pull away. Holding her in a side embrace, he sat in silence and took in the celestial wonders a bit longer.

"I can't let Hardy destroy my business. I almost wish I hadn't said anything to the tenure committee."

Her voice was barely audible, and he wasn't sure she'd meant for him to hear it. "You'd beat yourself up for the rest of your life if you hadn't. Maybe even wonder who else he'd hurt."

She sighed. "I would. So, you get it?"

"Suffering the consequences is easier than not being true to yourself."

Her face drew closer to his. "You really do get it."

"Yeah, because I'm the opposite. Since the grand theft auto thing, I've taken the blame for things I didn't do because it was easier." He hadn't spoken that truth to anyone. It lightened his load. Being the bad boy solved certain problems, but the good guy inside him had to carry around the lie. That falsehood constantly weighed on him.

She crinkled her nose, and her lower lip pouted just a bit. Adorable. Kissable.

"That doesn't make any sense."

"It's a pattern. When I try to break free, I fail." His voice cracked as the ever-present anger simmering below the surface threatened to erupt.

"That's not good for you or anybody else." She seemed to want to say more but closed her mouth and ducked her face from view.

"I'm working on it."

"Let me help you." Her tone seemed true. Not placation or empty.

"How can you do that?" He took his index finger and gently encouraged her to let him see her face.

"I'm not sure."

The flutter of her lush eyelashes enticed him. He let the backs of his fingers glide down her cheek. *So soft.* He brought his lips closer to hers. The instant pull back he expected didn't happen, so he leaned in closer. The heat of her marshmallow-sweet breath warmed him. He kept going. His lower lip met hers. Not yet a kiss, he stopped himself. *She's scared of Hardy. It's clouding her judgement. She won't be into me when she's safe.*

Her body fell against his, and it almost pushed him over the edge. *She'll kiss me when she's ready.* Allowing just a hint of his lip to brush against her, with a ragged gasp, he turned away.

A coyote howled in the distance. *I know how you feel, my friend.*

An engine revved to the north of them.

"Do you think that's the deputy chasing the shooter?" She stood, facing the sound.

He cradled her in his arms from behind. "I've got you. Silver or no. I've got you."

Chapter Five

The next day, Lainey finished her morning routine earlier than usual. She was less likely to think about the evocative feeling of Declan's lips near hers if she kept moving. Part of her couldn't wait to kiss him. Except she could make a long list of reasons why that wasn't a good idea, or at least it was bad timing.

She recalibrated her metal detector, left it in her tent, then checked on the core soil samples. Declan had already slipped away to his shaving tree, and Joan had headed south for a bit of privacy. Meanwhile, Andre repositioned boxes to store more supplies under the hardcover of his truck bed.

Unfortunately, the soil sample from the lake bottom still had too much moisture in it to allow it to be inspected. Desperate to find something proactive to do, she decided to review the maps one more time. Without thinking much about it, she ducked into her tent to retrieve the circular map canister.

Lainey looked left, then right. Where was it? She hadn't been sleepwalking when she got the detector and maps from the truck. Rolling her blankets out of the way, she found ... nothing. Frustrated, she scrambled around on her palms and knees, patting everything in sight. Nada.

With a quickening pulse and tension building in the muscles of her scalp, she flung the tent flap back and surveyed the ground. The heel mark of a boot lay before her in the dirt. *No. No. No.*

Not only had someone with a big foot been in her tent, the maps and her metal detector were missing. She crawled to the exit of the tent, then leaped over the entryway to avoid disturbing any footprints. Studying the ground, she followed the pointed toe of the boot's tracks to the rear of her tent and back into the woods.

With a shrill scream as if physical agony had racked her body, she crumpled to her knees and covered her face with her palms.

Andre reached her first. "Are you hurt? What's wrong?"

The strength of his grasp very welcome, she tried to stand. Her legs wobbled, and she collapsed against his chest.

She strained to hold back the flow of tears and whimpered, "Not me."

"Then who? What?" Andre's face contorted as he looked at her, searching for any injuries.

A rustling came from the bushes to the south. Running at full speed, clutching her unzipped shorts at the waist, Joan halted next to her. "What now?"

"It's gone." With a shaking arm, she pointed east.

Joan's head turned and bounced back. The look of concern on her face only made Lainey want to cry more.

"Take a breath and explain. Lainey, we need more." Andre supported her by the arms to steady her balance on her feet.

"He was here." It was as if time stood still while she waited for Andre to recognize who she meant by "he."

"That 'he'?" Andre asked. "The shooter 'he'?"

Nodding with fury, a tear slipped down her cheek. "He was in our tent."

Joan cupped her hands over her chest as if she wore no clothes. "That's creepy."

"Wait. The suspected shooter and now Peeping Tom has been how close to us?" Andre jerked to his full height.

Then, Declan burst onto their campsite with half his face still unshaven. "Peeping what?" he shouted, storming up to Andre, pounding his brother's shoulders, pushing him backwards. "The perp got the best of us on your guard duty."

"Stop that." Lainey darted between the brothers, placing her back against Andre's chest. "He guarded me well. We both looked away from the tents for like a minute. That's when the thief must've snuck into camp."

"This guy is a pro. Must have training. He can't be the professor." Declan raked his fingers through his disheveled hair, then his demeanor changed. "Sorry, Andre. Are we good?"

"You're forgiven, bro." Andre held up a clenched fist, and Declan met it with one of his own.

Lainey hated to break up the family moment. "Guys, he stole the maps and my best metal detector."

"What?" Declan's expression became a reddening scowl. He whipped out his phone from his back pocket and, with a few clicks, held it to his ear. "That's not harassment. That's theft. It's prosecutable."

"Let's take inventory to confirm if anything else is missing." Andre started toward his truck.

"Hello, this is off-duty officer Donnovan. I'd like to report a robbery." Declan twined his fingers with hers for just a second, then let go, mouthing, "You okay?"

She nodded once and went to console Joan, who'd gone pale.

About an hour later, a newer model, forest-green and tan sheriff's cruiser pulled up. The whirr of the engine's cooling fan kicked into high gear as a lady officer exited. This woman was brawny and tall. Lainey thought her five foot ten was lanky, but this deputy towered over her. Before she placed her hat on her head, Lainey noticed a few whisps of grey braided into her cornrows.

The cop shook her head. "A robbery now on top of everything else. Don't worry. I was brought up to speed during rollcall this morning."

Declan, Andre, and Joan filed into a line next to her like they were being inspected by a drill sergeant.

Lainey wouldn't want to take on this officer in a fistfight. She'd be knocked out with one punch, but it was a comfort to have this law professional on her side. "He's trying to ruin me."

Joan held up a case. "The stolen metal detector looks just like this one."

"I have video footage of the ladies using the two of them at once and of us looking at the maps in question," added Andre.

Declan chimed in. "I made the call and forwarded the shell casing for proper evidence documentation and chain of control."

The officer smiled. "You guys are making my job easier."

Joan leaned forward. "Have I seen you somewhere on TV?"

The deputy stood straighter as she faced Joan. "I played ball for the Lady Wolverines."

"Center, if I recall."

"That's right." The officer grinned widely, pulling in a deep breath.

Lainey's head swiveled toward Joan. Declan and Andre's expressions went slack.

Joan shrugged. "Can't a vertically challenged girl like basketball?"

Lainey laughed out loud. They all did. Leave it to Joan to break the tension. Again.

The officer completed the necessary electronic version of the forms before she photographed the remaining metal detector and footprints by Lainey's tent. "Let's hope no one else in my department needs to come out here again.

Something tells me you must be close to finding the treasure or this guy wouldn't be upping his game." She climbed back into her car and made her way toward the main road.

That comment made Lainey's day and terrified her at the same time. Every one of her brain cells shouted at her that she'd searched in the right area. But what would happen when she found the first piece of silver? She couldn't think about that, and thinking about kissing Declan was definitely off-limits.

With a less strained vibe in the camp, Lainey joined the crew for a late breakfast of cranberry bagels and cream cheese around the smoky ashes of the previous night's fire. "We won't be as efficient, but I say we carry on."

"I'm game," said Joan.

Declan and Andre seemed to slide back into business-as-usual mode, and a few minutes later, Lainey started the fifteen-minute hike toward the lake with the rest of the team behind her. They had decided to lock everything in the truck that wasn't coming with them. The tents stood empty. Lainey carried her most valuable tools with her. Even if she weren't using them, she wouldn't let them out of her sight.

Because she had the most experience with the metal detector, she assigned that job to herself. Joan and Declan shoveled up the silt on opposite sides where the stream met the lake, and Andre stood guard, hunting rifle at the ready.

A bank of clouds rolled in, and a slight drizzle fell. Not ideal conditions, but she wasn't going to let that stop her. She still held within her a deep-seated need to show Declan that her fieldwork skills would pass every quality standard.

Thoughts of Declan and the almost kiss made the gray around her darken. Joan said he was a good guy, but Mister Cop hadn't saved her from Hardy—or rather the guy Hardy must have hired. If he couldn't do that, maybe Joan was wrong. She certainly didn't trust herself to be a good judge of men.

He's a client and should be treated accordingly.

Joan came up to her and requested a break for lunch. With the clouds blocking out the sun, Lainey hadn't noticed how many hours had passed.

"You guys eat. Bring me a raspberry and almond energy bar. I want to keep working."

The ever-helpful Joan did as asked. When Lainey stood up to take a bite of her lunch, Declan waved at her, motioning for her to come eat with them. She shook her head and turned her back so she couldn't be distracted. *My work is my priority. I can't let myself get involved with a man. Declan's not good for me.*

The man in her thoughts trotted up. "It's okay to take a break. No one seems to be bothering us. Come and eat with me. I mean us."

"Thanks for your concern. I don't want to let your mother down. I have a business to think of as well." She gave him a forced smile.

He gave her a slight grin in return, but it didn't include the display of dimples she'd come to enjoy.

* * *

The drizzle let up, and a sliver of sun snuck through the heavy clouds as Declan made his way back under a tree alongside the stream. He didn't know what bee had gotten into Lainey's bonnet. Was she mad that he'd allowed the guy stalking her for Hardy to steal the metal detector? It probably wasn't some random thief. The dig site was so remote no one else would know Lainey's tent had valuable items to steal. He wasn't even on guard duty. Can't a guy get a shave with a bit of privacy?

This whole thing was only supposed to be a short treasure hunt. It had been all he and his brothers figured they could afford. Maybe the stress of trying to find the silver raised her agitation? Making a video to entertain his mom was the focus of the trip. If the footage got her to giggle or smile, he'd be happy. But to find the silver beavers would be amazing, even if some lowlife was out there trying to slow any progress made by Lainey's treasure hunting company.

Biting into his minty energy bar with vigor, Declan's mind drifted back to having Lainey in his arms, the twinkling stars overhead. The almost kiss. Could she be pouting because he'd made a romantic gesture too soon? Or did she want him to kiss her, and because that kind of didn't happen, she was frustrated? Women. He couldn't figure them out. Perhaps this trip wasn't the best time to try.

Andre burst into a long string of laughter at something Joan had said, and Declan did his best to play along. Joan seemed to be the glue that kept Lainey together. Having her tag along was a blessing. A pang of guilt thumped around in his head for having been so penny-pinching. If he'd known then what he recognized now, he'd have paid for her food out of his pocket whether his brothers approved or not.

"Did you catch the size of that beaver hauling the massive branch? That thing's stronger than I am." Joan chuckled some more.

"Yeah, I wouldn't want to get thwacked by his tail. It'd leave a mark," replied Andre.

Determined to enjoy the day, Declan tossed out what he thought was a funny comment. "Earlier, I picked up the blackest, hardest piece of dirt I've ever held. I launched it back into the stream like a fish too small to keep." An honest smile emerged on his face. His inner gloom began to clear. "It caused a big splash. I should've used it like a skipping rock and seen how many hops I could get."

Neither Joan nor Andre seemed to glean the humor. So, he took another bite and observed the speed of the passing storm clouds.

The wind, however, must have carried his voice just right. Lainey barreled at him with her earphones hanging around her neck. "You threw it back. Why would you do that without showing it to me?"

"I thought it was a rock or something." A little voice in his head started to tell him he'd screwed up royally this time, but there was no need to take on blame he didn't deserve.

"The silver beaver tokens are about two inches long." She held her thumb and index finger at about that length and shook them in front of his face. "Could your black dirt have been about that long?"

"Maybe." His last swallow of power bar landed in his stomach, splashing acid, causing heartburn. She hadn't specifically accused him of anything, but the way she asked the question bruised his ego. He faulted her for not having taken a more subtle approach. She had the Ph.D.

Lainey grabbed the sleeve of his t-shirt, urging him to his feet. "Show me where you threw it."

"Easy. I'm not the professional treasure hunter here. It's not like I've had *eight years* of college. You didn't tell any of us what to look for. You just said to look." He yanked his shirt free from her fist. Immediately regretting it, he wanted to back down and apologize. His inner demon wouldn't let him.

The bad boy he'd so often forced himself to be had taken control.

"Common sense would tell you. You should've shown it to me." She got in his face, then jabbed two fingers through his belt loop. Turning toward the stream, she hauled him with her and used her other arm to point at the soft flow of water. "Show me."

Andre jumped into the fray. "That's a little over the top. Let go of his shorts."

"I've got this." Declan didn't need his little brother coming to his rescue.

Lainey must not have liked the two against one odds. "Andre, if you've finished eating, stand guard."

He couldn't decipher what she said next. All he caught was a jumble of words as he, along with everyone else, raised their voices, trying to get their point across.

"Silence!" Joan surprised him by having the strongest pair of lungs. Then she whispered, "Let's not tell the shooter guy we found a piece of the treasure."

"Is that what we did?" His thoughts swirled, making him dizzy.

First, Lainey's and then Joan's heads furiously nodded.

"Oh." He closed his eyes and covered his ears, blocking out his senses to better concentrate his focus. *Where was I standing?* Nothing he tried worked. "I was on the same side of the stream as the tree where the bullet ricocheted." That's all he could remember.

Lainey raced over to a duffel bag, retrieved a pair of knee-high rain boots, then stuffed in her feet, shoes and all. "I'm going to start upstream and work my way to the lake. This top-of-the-line baby is waterproof." She waved her detector high up in the air.

Declan asked, "What do you want me to do?"

"Stand guard with Andre." Her clipped response smacked him in the face.

More like get out of your way. I'm no help to you. He couldn't let himself celebrate the potential of finding the silver. With a sigh, he secured the holster of his service weapon around his waist and strolled over to Andre on the opposite side of the stream to discuss setting a perimeter for each of them to monitor.

Joan kicked off her shoes and started searching in the stream barefooted. He could have done that. Well, he'd messed up once already. Maybe he'd better stick to being part of the security detail. He could excel at that.

It seemed like hours passed. He hadn't eaten much for lunch, and his energy level began to wane. Another batch of angry clouds gathered toward the south, and the northerly breeze told him he'd be getting wet again soon. Andre could endure it. He wasn't sure about the ladies.

Cupping his hands around his mouth, he shouted toward the stream. "Hey, let's call it a day. We need to drive to town to get ice for the coolers and prepare for a wet night."

Joan motioned for Lainey to take off her headset and pointed at the blackening clouds. Lainey's shoulders dropped, and he wanted to pull her into a hug. She'd worked hard. Harder than any of them. He'd found a new respect for her abilities, and she could rough it. He'd been wrong to doubt her.

The wind whipped up, and high weeds thrashed at the exposed skin of his legs all the way back to camp. Miserable conditions. Bad went to worse as he pushed through the last bit of brush to the camp's clearing.

Both tents were flat. His heart sank. Had the strong, straight-line winds pulled the stakes up from the ground? Dropping all he carried, he ran to his tent and, squatting with one knee on the ground, tugged on the rope. It flipped in the air. No resistance from the stake. The rope had been cut. With quick strides, he raced to all four corners. Every piece of rope he could see had a clean, man-made cut. Clenching his jaw, he ignored the cramping of the muscles in his back.

How could I have let this happen? I should've had Andre guard the camp while I protected Lainey.

"You've got to be kidding me." The strained sound of Andre's voice told him there was more bad news.

He rounded his brother's truck to join the others where they stood, mouths agape. The shooter-thief had upped his game yet again. The sliced ropes were child's play. The back window on the driver's side of Andre's truck had been shattered. And more importantly, every door and even the truck's bed cap were open.

He shook his head in dismay. His earlier thought of not being a good leader because he hadn't asked Andre to guard the camp reared up, sucking the breath from his lungs. He'd made another mistake and had no business being a cop. How could he have let down his younger brother, Joan, and Lainey. The possibility of giving his mother a gift just ceased.

Lainey will never want to date me now. Why would she?

His training and instincts took over. But would that be enough? "Let's patch the window with my duffel bag, gather everything of value, and decide our next action."

"I'm so sorry," Lainey said. "I'll pay for the damages."

The saddened expression on her face stabbed him in the heart. Physical discomfort he could endure, but witnessing her emotional pain was more than he could withstand. He wanted to take on her suffering and carry it for her. But how?

Chapter Six

How could I let this happen? I drove Dr. Hardy to seek revenge, and now I may lose my business because of it.

Declan ran to check the damage while Andre rushed to his truck. Still carrying a heavy load of equipment, Lainey stumbled toward the vehicle. It took her a few seconds to realize all the doors and truck bed had been opened by someone while she hunted for the treasure. Andre began shouting. The frantic sound of his voice reached her, but she didn't comprehend the words. A numbness came over her, along with a heavy sense of doom.

When it became apparent the vandal had shattered Andre's back window, she offered to pay for damages. It was like an out-of-body experience. She was in charge. Why wasn't she leading? The clouds in her mind grew darker than the ones overhead. The rain that had chased them to camp finally fell in big drops that became sheets of water as the wind pushed them. Puddles formed, and water gathered into little rivers that rushed downhill toward the lake.

Declan barked orders. Next actions or something.

Mindlessly, she gathered all the gear, everything everyone else had dropped when they'd first came upon the destruction.

"The bedding is missing," called out Andre.

Joan added, "He took our food, too."

"All of our suitcases and even Andre's toolbox. Everything's gone."

Declan's last cry of woe did her in. She wasn't sad; she was angry. Anger made her cry. She couldn't let anyone see that. Facing away from the truck, tears streamed down her face along with the mammoth raindrops. Hiding that she had caved to her emotions was the rain's only benefit.

I'll track him back to where he took our stuff. A brilliant thought until she looked down at her feet. The rain had already washed away her latest footprint left in the moistening dirt. She turned a circle, looking for any sort of clue about the direction their supplies had been taken. No tire marks. No ruts of a wagon's wheel. All washed away. The tall grasses changed direction with every new gust of wind. An attempt to track the thief would be a waste of time.

Pulling inside herself, she assessed the situation. No food, no shelter, no clothing, except for what was on their backs or had been carried to the lake.

Even her soil samples had been jumbled into a pile of dirt that wouldn't be useful to her at all. It wouldn't be enough. *No one will ever hire me again. I've failed to keep my brother's dreams of treasure hunting alive.* She swiped at her face as if to brush the rain from her eyes.

Declan worked to secure his duffel bag over the busted window to block the water as she approached him from behind. "I'm canceling this treasure hunt. I'll give you a full refund."

He whirled on her. *He'll never try to kiss me again. I wouldn't be worthy even if he did. He has every right to hate me.*

Joan charged at her from the opposite side of the truck, splashing mud in all directions with every stomping stride. "We're so close. We can overcome this setback. Don't let Hardy win."

The lump forming in Lainey's throat blocked her words.

Andre piled on. "I've got insurance. It's just stuff."

Declan's next comment put everything into perspective. "My mom hasn't quit on life, and I'm not going to quit on her. Videoing this hunt for her continues."

She wasn't sure what meant more to her, that no one had blamed her or that everyone wanted to continue. "We need to restock."

"We should stay here until an updated report has been filed. I'll call the sheriff." Declan searched the pile she'd made. "Let's get everything we have out of the rain."

She darted toward her metal detector. It was the best tool they had left. Within a minute, everything, even the tents, were stored under the lid of the truck bed. Lainey brushed the broken glass from the interior and sat on the least comfortable seat before anyone could say otherwise. The guys climbed into the front, and Joan piled in beside her. As her friend lightly stroked her forearm, Lainey sat in silence. Drops of rain on her skin gathered one into another and rolled down her arms and legs. *What would my father do? What would Frank do?*

It seemed like hours, but only minutes passed before the deputy from this morning pulled up. Declan jumped out and ran to meet her. He ducked into her car while she waited with Joan and Andre. The rain began to ease, and by the time Declan returned, it had ceased altogether.

"Well, there's bad news and more bad news." Declan got back in the passenger seat as the deputy drove away.

Andre half chuckled, acting like a comedian with a cigar doing his act. "Give us the worst of the news first."

Lainey managed to join him with a grin.

"We think Hardy hired someone to get his revenge, but we have no proof. From the local law's perspective, any opportunistic lowlife could have stolen our belongings." Declan turned in the seat to allow her to see his face. "Sorry."

Before she could thank him for his honesty, Joan mimicked Andre's performance with one of her own. "So, give us the better bad news."

"There isn't a store open this late that carries all the things we need on this island, but the deputy told me about a motel with a restaurant about a fifteen-minute drive west of here."

"We can shop in the morning." Lainey did her best to sound positive.

Joan nodded. "Hopefully, the motel has a hair dryer."

"You had me at restaurant." Andre started his truck.

The motel would be lucky to earn one star, but it had vacancies and a roof. Lainey booked two rooms with double beds. She then volunteered to get take-out pizzas. Meanwhile Declan, Andre, and Joan did their best to spread the tents and other bags out across the various open spaces on the floor inside the rooms so they could dry. The Italian spices in the pizza sauce were better than she expected. With food in her stomach and somewhat drier clothes on, she sat on a plastic chair by the motel's small rectangular pool. The blue light on the side of the deep end shimmered as the water moved past it. Staring at the wavy beams, she drifted into a daydream.

Crickets chirped, and the waning moon peered out from behind passing clouds. The scent of fresh rain still filled the air. Even after the cooling precipitation, the night remained a warm and muggy midsummer's night. She continued to battle within herself. How easily I became a quitter. That's not the real me. A youthful couple with energetic children set up on the opposite side of the pool. A tow-haired boy did a cannonball. It reminded her of when she played with her brother. Frank loved getting her wet with that stunt. Since she'd started her treasure-hunting business to honor him, she had to find a way to carry on. No, she needed to succeed.

"I have a plan," said Declan out of the blue. "You're not going to like it."

His voice brought her back to the present.

"I'm listening." Something about his tone made her uneasy.

Declan leaned forward, his elbows on his knees. "I want to set a trap for the jerk who Hardy hired. He's bound to make a mistake."

"Until Hardy destroys my career like I did his, he's going to keep coming after me. Finding the treasure will make that harder for him." Lainey had let down her wet locks to let them air dry, so she pulled her fingers through them like a comb.

"Perfect. Then I'll nab this guy, bring him to justice, and then Hardy." Declan seemed to have it all figured out.

Lainey chose to concentrate on what she could control. Finding the silver beaver tokens became even more important. Pushing the thief from her mind, she focused her grey matter on creating a strategy of her own.

* * *

Early the next morning, Declan loved feeling clean after his hot shower. Then he had to put back on the clothes from yesterday that he'd decided to use as pajamas. Something about the texture of the sheets told him that was a prudent idea. He wondered how the ladies fared in their rustic lodgings. At least in the tents they had their own sleeping bags, not some strange lumpy bed with worn-out elastic on the fitted sheet.

The thought of some hired gun having his pillow and other stuff made the muscles in his jaw go tight. He didn't care if he injured Lainey's pride today. He would take charge. Well, over everything not specific to searching for the silver. She seemed to be off in another world lately, anyway. No way a guy could figure out what women were thinking or when the winds of change would have him tangled in their next batch of thoughts.

At breakfast, he ordered the hungry man's platter and suggested the others eat hearty as well. "Today is going to be eventful. I can feel it in every cell of my body."

Andre and Joan seemed lost making their own itinerary. Everyone had their faces glued to fully charged phones, instead of enjoying conversation with each other. The aftermath of yesterday's robbery was still sinking into his brain. Maybe that was true of everyone else.

"I vote to have Andre and Joan do the shopping after Lainey and I get dropped off at the lake to continue the hunt." He waited for pushback. None came. Instead, he noticed a couple of head nods. Was he talking to himself?

"I found a dealership. I'm chatting online to see if they have a window in stock. If they do, Joan and I can head there and then go shopping." Andre went back to typing.

Joan met his gaze. "I know Lainey's sizes. I'm assuming Andre knows yours. Do you have any food requests?"

"I trust you," replied Declan, waiting for Lainey to join the conversation.

Without lifting her head from her plate, she said, "I've made a to-do list for myself." Then she shoved another fork full of scrambled eggs into her mouth.

Words. She'd spoken words to him. It was the first thing she'd said directed at him all morning. Had she put him back in the doghouse? One minute, she almost let him kiss her. The next, she became all cerebral and cool toward him. Why did he want her to become his girlfriend so much? That was the truth of it. He wanted her to himself, committed, monogamous. Currently, her aloofness had his head spinning. That, too, would pass. He'd have her to himself all morning.

After breakfast, repacking their gear—what little was left of it—didn't take long. Before they left the parking lot, he gave a command. "I want to set up a new camp. Close to the lake, but on the highest ground we can find."

"You mean like Lainey wanted on our first day?" Joan had an innocent lilt in her voice.

She was Lainey's best friend. He gave her props for defending Lainey's intelligence, but throwing his tactical error in his face still stung. He ignored the insult. Instead, he gave himself a pat on the back for having learned. He could evolve. If he had any chance at winning or keeping Lainey's interest, he figured he'd be evolving some more. That thought sucked the air out of his lungs. His bad boy persona could deal with it. The real Declan swallowed hard.

As directed, Andre pulled off the main road closer to the lake. When they'd stopped for gas, Declan had filled the cooler with ice and food to last him and Lainey until supper. He had his cell, service weapon, and Andre's hunting rifle. Lainey had her mobile phone and a trusty metal detector. Two people in the middle of nowhere with not much between them, and a hired gun after them. They'd be fine.

LAINEY SHEA'S TREASURE QUEST: THE SILVER BEAVER TOKENS

No sooner had Andre turned his truck around, Lainey marched into the water, headset on and metal detecting wand waving.

"You want to clue me in?" He threw his palm in the air like he'd thrown a challenge flag in pro football.

How can I get her to pay attention to me? "Hey, Lainey. Please respond."

Her shoulders slumped, and she turned toward him. "I hunt. You stand guard." Then she gave him a swift chin lift, and the wand started moving from side to side in front of her.

So much for winning her over. How could he if she insisted on wearing that darn headset the entire time? He temporarily leaned the shotgun against a tree and put his phone on selfie mode. With himself in the bottom corner, he videoed Lainey in the lake. "Hi, Mom. We're hard at work here. Check Lainey out. She has a hunch. We'll be bringing you those beavers soon enough. Love you."

Having made progress on the main reason for the trip, Declan walked the perimeter. Maybe the hired thug thought he'd gotten the better of Lainey when the crew packed up everything and left last night. Or he may have come to the lake one last time. Then, instead of it being one against four, it would be one against two. That made a chill run down his spine.

Every wisp of wind had him twitching. A squirrel skittered across a branch, and he raised the rifle to fire. He'd left his sunglasses in camp yesterday. He didn't even have a ball cap to shade his face. Standing in the increasing heat didn't help. Sweat ran down his back and into his eyes.

Lainey seemed to have the right idea. She looked cooler in the water. His gym shoes had already seen better days. Lainey had trudged into the lake wearing hiking boots, and if she gave those up for the cause, he could ante up a pair of sneakers.

Hours passed. Lainey's maneuvers kept her in a tight pattern in the shallow water. With his eyes peeled toward the shore, he did the same about four or five feet from her.

A big rustling in the grass drew his attention. This was not a squirrel. A moment later, it happened again, only this time closer. It's a rabbit, he told himself. As if being rushed by a predator, the sound intensified.

Declan raised the rifle, fully prepared to fire. He pointed his scope into the swaying area of grass.

"What do you hear? Who is it?"

The shrill tone of Lainey's voice made his blood run cold. He'd let no one hurt her. If he was worthy of being a cop, he would prevail.

He risked a side glance at her. The headset was now around her neck.

"Stay behind me," he shouted.

The warmth of her palm in the center of his back startled him, then pleased him. When she followed his orders, he could protect her. He inched toward the shore. The slosh of his soggy shoes hit dry land.

If the grass sways an inch, I'll fire a warning shot. He eased his finger to the trigger. The biggest flurry of grass yet shifted directly in front of him. He exhaled for a steadier shot.

"What are you doing? You can't shoot yet."

"My decision. Stay back."

"What if it's an animal?"

Just then, the rustling in the grass retreated in a hurry.

He lowered his weapon. "I was going to fire a warning shot. Only if necessary. Do you mind? I'm the cop and your security guard. Remember?"

"Wait. Stop talking." She repositioned the headset back over her ears.

The woman could be infuriating. How could he explain if she wasn't willing to listen? "Do you want me to protect you or not?"

"Can you please be quiet? I got a hit." She smiled at him.

It took Declan a second to process what that meant. Then, the beep grew louder and faster. Even he couldn't miss it. She found metal. He held his breath and bit his tongue. She hadn't yet gone back to hunting, but her machine had still been active. It must be more sensitive than he'd imagined.

"Hold this." She heaved the detector in his direction.

Swinging the rifle over his shoulder, he grabbed the device. Lainey pulled a small rake-like tool from her belt and thrust it into the shin-deep water. Then, she bent at the waist and dug around with her fingers.

She popped up so fast she nearly caught him under the chin with her head. She'd clawed up a ball of soot. Slowly, she peeled back some plant life, then some decaying leaves and a bunch of brown mud.

He'd thought she might be repulsed by the dirt. Add that to the list of preconceived notions he'd had about her that were wrong. She practically played with the goo.

Then, as quickly as she straightened, she stooped again. This time, she waved her arm through the top couple of inches of water.

The look she gave him was magical. In filthy clothes, with her hair in a knot on top of her head and no makeup, she'd never been more beautiful.

"I can't wait for Joan to get back from the store." She grinned.

"Why?"

"Because I need silver cleaner." She held up a black oblong object still covered in small clumps of debris.

He blinked, wiped the sweat from his eyes, and looked again. "You think so?"

"I do," she shouted.

In an instant, she leaped and threw her arms around his neck. Her face now inches above his, he wrapped one arm around her torso, tossed the detector onto the grass, and encircled her caboose with the other. It didn't matter how hot he was, he welcomed her added heat. Then her glorious mouth came closer to his. Before he could wet his lips, hers made contact, sharing the strawberry taste of her favorite hard candy.

Soft, gliding eagerness. He kissed her back, unleashing all the passion he'd tamped down for days. He explored her mouth with his. Striding away from the shore, he set her down on the silty beach. Then he hauled her into a hug, pressing every inch of his body to hers. The rosy scent of the motel's shampoo filled his nostrils. Bending her back a bit, he dropped the rifle onto some tall grass. Freed from the gun strap, he found the binding that contained her curls and sent her long locks sailing on the breeze. Threading his fingers into the hair he adored, he dove into another deep kiss. Eventually, he pulled back and pecked her on the cheek one last time.

"I hope you've been longing for that as much as me," he whispered, his words thick with desire.

The corners of her lips pulled into a smile. "I have."

The crackle of tires against gravel on the road's berm kept him from giving her another smooch. He hoped the sound meant the approach of Andre or maybe a patrol car.

Lainey took one swift backward stride and, yanking her ribbon from him, gathered her hair to confine its beauty once again. She picked up the detector and faced the approaching sound. His body shivered. He wanted her warmth back, her lips. At least Lainey had found something promising, and the perp had left them in peace.

Shading his eyes with his palm, Declan recognized Andre's truck with Joan in the front passenger seat. The noise grew louder. Could it be the officer accompanying Andre? A second vehicle followed the truck. Not a cruiser. A blue SUV. A Toyota. Exactly like the one his father drove. His backbone stiffened, and his jaw clamped shut. It was his father. Plus, his older brother. Andre may have thought he'd brought the cavalry. Wait until he gave this little bro a piece of his mind.

Lainey had found some silver. The hired perp hadn't struck this morning. Things were looking up. So, why did he have such a strong sense of dread?

Chapter Seven

From the look on Declan's face, it was clear he wasn't pleased about the SUV that followed Andre's truck. Honestly, she had her own composure to think about. She had kissed him. What on earth had possessed her to do that? Physically, the smooch was divine. Her body liked every second of it. Career-wise, it was a bad decision. She thought about staying in touch so that, after she no longer considered him a client, she could ask him to join a group event to see if the attraction remained alive.

Unable to undo the past, she'd have to see how he acted toward her. Hopefully, he'd still give her a good review as a treasure hunter. One silver beaver wasn't a treasure, but her experience told her she could find more if given the chance. Struggling to contain her curls back in the ribbon without a mirror, she did her best to look presentable for the visitors. Meeting potential new customers wearing yesterday's clothes was not ideal. She sighed and put on a passable smile.

Andre rolled down his window. When Declan approached, she tagged along, the tarnished beaver in her palm.

"What did you do? Call home for help? You brought Dad?" The tension in Declan's face was obvious as he spewed the words in a hiss.

I'm about to meet Declan's dad looking like this? So much for making a good first impression.

Andre pitched his sunglasses on the dash. "Bro, chill. I've been texting Hugo updates. He invested in this project, too, and deserved to know if the gift for Mom would be good."

Oh, right. Hugo was the third Donnovan brother.

"I get that, but ... Dad?"

Andre put an index finger over his mouth and then began to whisper. "I'm as surprised as you are. Last night, I texted Hugo that I'd found a dealership to get the truck fixed. Before the mechanic finished with my window, he showed up with Dad."

"Geez." Declan whirled around, thumped his back against the truck, and crossed his arms over his chest.

"You should see all the gear he brought. Dad doesn't camp. It's more like glamping."

Joan had exited the truck. Standing beside her, she gave Lainey a side glance. "Greaaaat ... family drama."

Lainey decided to lighten the mood. She held up the black hunk of what she hoped was silver. "I found this."

Joan let out a girly scream and hugged her. When she started jumping up and down, Lainey jumped along. She needed to release some excess energy.

"What's all the excitement about?" A white-haired man about Declan's height and build came up from behind Andre's truck.

"Hi, Dad. This is Lainey Shea. She found part of the treasure." Declan gave his dad a brief, one-shouldered hug, and his father gave him one pat on the back.

At least, Declan had given her full credit and had almost been welcoming to his father.

She displayed the beaver as if it were priceless. "I need to use some silver cleaner."

"Coming right up." Joan trotted to the other side of Andre's truck.

Mr. Donnovan pulled his key ring from his pocket. Fidgeting with it, he found the item he sought and scraped the blackened oval. True to form, the shine of silver shown through the tarnish.

"Would you look at that? It's definitely metal." Mr. Donnovan gave her a wide smile, and the dimples she had expected showed themselves. "Call me Colin. We're informal in this family."

"Yes, sir. Colin, sir." She pulled the beaver away from him. "I'll video the Donnovan men setting up camp, so you can all be in it together."

"Who's taking care of mom?" Declan's eyebrows furrowed together.

"Relax, son. Three or four neighbors are looking in on her. She enjoys the company." Colin meandered back to his SUV as if he didn't have a care in the world.

Hugo, the tallest and brawniest Donnovan, marched up. He had on a police Kevlar vest, an AR-15 slung over his shoulder, and completed his ensemble with pistols on both sides of his gun belt. "No one messes with my brothers. Where shall I stand guard?"

"Hugo, Lainey. Lainey, Hugo."

LAINEY SHEA'S TREASURE QUEST: THE SILVER BEAVER TOKENS

That was as much of an intro as Declan permitted. Instead of letting her chat with his oldest brother, he led Hugo back to where the noise had been in the underbrush.

I have a protection detail made of four officers of the law. I should feel safe, but I don't. Her gaze circled the lake to see if she could spot the reflection of what she figured to be a pair of binoculars. Nothing out of the ordinary came into view.

Now that she'd found the first beaver, she needed to make a claim on the find before Dr. Hardy found some silver as well and tried to steal her accomplishment as his own.

Before she could reach for her phone, Joan approached her with a plastic bowl, silver cleaner, and a cheap toothbrush. In a matter of minutes, Lainey had scrubbed off the tarnish and other debris to find a gleaming beaver-like token. Identical to the ones she'd seen in pictures. It warmed her heart.

Using Joan's palm as a specimen tray, she photographed the metal, along with a ruler, from every angle. She'd already contacted the Hudson's Bay Company History Foundation in hopes that she'd find the treasure. Now, she emailed the pictures to a historian who could provide a preliminary corroboration of the find, pending seeing the token in person. *Take that, Dr. Hardy.*

With that all important task complete, she made a point of finding Declan. While taking the pics, her stomach had growled loudly. To her surprise, it was well past lunchtime and neither she nor Declan had eaten anything since breakfast.

She found him a few moments later. He'd busied himself, pounding stakes into the ground to hold up the two tents Joan had purchased with Lainey's company's credit card.

"Can you take a lunch break with me? I'd like to strategize on the search grid." That sounded businesslike enough. No one needed to know that she'd kissed him.

"Sounds good to me. I'm starved." He followed her to sit atop a boulder.

She liked this spot, because it gave her the best view of the lake and stream. The pine trees behind her provided shade, and the scent reminded her of the holidays with her parents. Fluffy clouds overhead gathered into what her imagination considered to be fun shapes like pillows or cotton balls.

The lunchmeat hoagie that Joan had brought back for her tasted better than any sandwich she'd ever eaten. The aroma of fresh baked bread and the creaminess of the melted provolone cheese soothed her craving for comfort food. Declan seemed equally ravenous. While he devoured his lunch, it gave her the opportunity to talk.

"About before. The adrenaline rush. I'm not sure why I—well, can we keep things professional? At least until we get back to Ohio." She hoped she'd made her point without discounting her attraction to him or hurting his feelings.

"Sure. With my father here, I'm going to act differently than you've ever seen me behave before. Don't take it personally." He took another huge bite of his lunch and didn't glance in her direction.

"About that. Your father, I mean. Maybe if the two of you search for more beavers together, you can rekindle your bond." She held her breath and hoped she hadn't encroached on his privacy.

He turned his head as if to check to see Hugo's field search revealed any clues about the mysterious rustling in the brush. "Stay out of it."

"Roger that." A policewoman she was not, though trying on the lingo for size tickled her funny bone. It didn't become her. Maybe she wouldn't fit in with all these officers. She was an academic by trade, after all.

"I'm guessing, after the camp is secured, we might get in another two hours of treasure hunting. Honestly, I don't think we're going to find a bunch of silver beavers all clumped together. I know they were most likely hidden together, but after two hundred years of winter freezes and spring thaws—"

"Hugo, Andre, and I can secure the perimeter. Tell us where you're going to search."

"What about your dad?"

"Dad does what Dad wants. No matter what. That'll quickly become clear to you." He laughed, but it wasn't an "I'm enjoying myself" kind of chuckle.

"Okay. Good talk." She ate the rest of her hoagie in silence.

When she was finished, he stood and pulled her to her feet.

"Please, come back to camp with me. No one goes anywhere alone." He put his palm in the small of her back and gently guided her off their perch, then he suddenly leaned away from her as if she had cooties. The abrupt reaction made her wince, though keeping up professional pretenses had been her request.

Declan went back to putting up the tents. Joan still worked with Andre, deciding which items to leave in the truck and what to put around the new firepit, which had been constructed to Colin's exacting specifications.

She designated herself as the videographer. Creating too much footage shouldn't be a problem. Andre would be the editor. She took cameo footage of each person. Then realizing she hadn't gotten any footage of Hugo, she wandered to the edge of camp. When she used her fingers to increase the screen's magnification to get a close-up of him, she noticed a flash of light—a reflection of some kind. What was that?

Putting the phone's camera on its highest resolution, she scanned the trees above Hugo's head on the other upward-sloping bank. There it was again. She caught the image and held perfectly still. Apparently, the individual who'd been harassing them hadn't given up.

"Declan. Come here. Like now." She kept her voice even and low, then tilted the camera as if she was none the wiser.

Acting a bit distracted, Declan did as she'd asked. "What?"

"Don't make a big deal out of this." She trembled, apparently enough for him to notice. It couldn't be helped. Fear gripped her every cell.

That wrenched his attention into focus. "The perp is nearby, isn't he?" He squinted his eyes. "Where?"

* * *

Continuing to face Lainey, Declan took a few steps to nonchalantly put himself between her and the bad guy. He'd protect her if it was the only good thing he did on this trip.

"He's at my twelve o'clock about twenty yards up the hill." Lainey squared her shoulders in a specific direction.

"You and Joan stay with my dad, then send Andre to me."

Declan kept tabs on her over the next minute or so as she spoke to his father and waved for Hugo to join him. *I'd rather have my brothers with me on this mission.* Unfortunately, his father came with Andre.

Lainey mouthed, "Sorry."

She didn't have to apologize. He understood just how stubborn his dad could be.

"What's this? Leave the ladies with your over-the-hill father? I think not." His father's jaw was set, and he leaned in toward Declan to make his point beyond clear.

Andre intervened, his expression sincere. "Lainey's the most important part of this operation. We need the guy with the highest skill level to keep her safe, Dad."

How did he know just what to say and how to say it?

With a swift salute and a proud stride, his father went back toward the tents. Lainey and Joan hopped on whatever orders his father must have given. A flurry of activity ensued around the campsite. Declan couldn't think about that now.

Relaying the suspected location of the thief, he asked Hugo and Andre to head toward the road and then circle back to surprise the hired gun from behind. "Joan and Dad can stay by the trucks while Lainey and I continue to hunt. We need this guy to think we have no idea he's near."

His brothers complied and did a good acting job. As they meandered behind Andre's truck, they kept talking and pointing at trees on the bank of the lake in the opposite direction of the suspected thief's position.

Earlier, when he and Andre raised the tents, Andre had suggested putting their phones on silent and installing a tracking app. That way the three brothers would know the location of the others if another attack forced them to scatter. A quick view of the screen showed two circles on the map moving toward the road. It gave him peace of mind. Now, he just needed to convince his father to stay put. As he moved back toward the tents, Joan was by the fire, so he stopped next to her. "Did you get ground beef and buns at the store? My dad makes the best flame-grilled burgers I've ever tasted."

Joan responded with a nod.

"Great. Lainey and I should keep hunting, so everything looks normal. Joan, could you please help my father make supper for us all?"

This time, Joan gave him a knowing grin and a hidden wink. With a bit of teamwork, he had a chance of retaining some semblance of control over what could be a dangerous situation. Giving a gift to his mom wouldn't be worth it if someone got injured.

With a plan in motion, Declan escorted Lainey back to where she'd found the beaver. Due to Lainey's quality standards, Joan had opted not to purchase any machines available in the local store. The lone professional grade wand they still had would be worlds better than several low quality and less expensive detectors. He stood guard on the bank, while Lainey waded into the water, staying a little closer to the shore.

The pattern of this morning became the norm again. Grateful for the ball cap and sunglasses Andre had purchased for him earlier, he sent him a mental thank you. Lainey looked a bit ridiculous with the floppy-brimmed hat Joan had brought back for her. It also made it more difficult for him to gaze at her beautiful face without her knowing it, though he had to push romantic thoughts of her away. He needed to stay focused, listen for movement on the hillside, and be ready to protect.

He monitored her as she made her way upstream, the detector constantly moving from side to side. Crossing over the water, he confirmed no sniper rifle's laser had been pointed at her like it had on their first day. Maybe having the local law regularly showing up deterred the vandal from striking again.

He'd almost relaxed when a rapid flurry of heavy footfalls and thrashing grass occurred in the location where Lainey had previously spotted the reflection of the binocular lenses. Wrapping his arms around her, he snatched her up and ducked behind the nearest large tree. She didn't say a word, but her eyes grew as big as saucers.

According to the app on his phone, Hugo and Andre converged on the same location. The spice of the pepperjack cheese in his lunch soured his stomach. A heated breeze carried a whiff of his perspiration to his nose. He yearned to be beside his brothers, but his priority had to be Lainey's safety. A pounding began in his head as he waited.

"Clear," shouted Hugo.

Andre replied with a normal voice, "All clear. Declan, you can come out."

Lainey had lowered her headset. Declan held her against the tree for continued safety and took a quick peek around the tree. His brothers made their way through some thick underbrush to meet him. He immediately raised his rifle toward the other side of the stream. This hired thug had skills. He couldn't allow himself to be set up in a trap. The stillness all around him unnerved him.

"Dad. Everything okay in camp? Is Joan with you?" Declan shouted with such volume it left a ringing sensation in his ears.

Waiting for a response, he gave Lainey another once over for a laser's red circle. Nothing.

When no response came, he took off at a full sprint, grabbing Lainey by the arm yanking her along with him. She carried the detector as she ran, the hat flopping in the breeze. His unencumbered brothers raced to the tents before him, but he wouldn't leave his partner behind. Safety before speed. A fire blazed in the pit, but no one was in sight.

"Dad!" It hurt his throat he screamed with such intensity.

Lainey broke free and darted toward her tent. "Joan!"

Declan raced after her, hot on Lainey's tail. His brothers scattered, calling out. He searched one tent after another. Andre rounded his truck, and Hugo ran toward his father's vehicle.

Hugo came back, his head jerking and eyes protruding. "You wouldn't believe ..."

All laughs and smiles, his dad, along with Joan, strolled back into camp. "What? I made a video call to your mom using the SUV's screen. I introduced her to Joan." He wandered over to the pit to stoke the fire. "She's fine. Your mother."

Joan shook her head and at least had the decency to show a bit of remorse. "The A/C was on high, and the call's sound was even louder. Sorry. Hugo said you shouted, but we couldn't hear you."

His dad scratched his stubbled chin. "What time do you want to eat? I can have burgers ready in twenty minutes." Seemingly oblivious to the panic he'd caused, his father didn't wait for an answer as he moseyed back to the cooler on the tailgate of Andre's truck.

Lainey's gaze cut to Declan. "I see what you mean. Thanks for the heads up." It pleased him that she managed to laugh at the situation.

That seemed to put his brothers at ease, but he was still on high alert. "Report. Evidence. Anything?"

"The guy's getting careless," Hugo replied. "He left a rectangular, plastic tarp lying on the ground. Neither of us touched it."

"Not like we can tie it to the rest of the incidents. I followed his footprint for a couple of feet. It looked like he climbed a tree or something. He's still one move ahead of us." With a heavy sigh, Andre secured his weapons in his truck and went to help with the cooking.

Declan pulled Hugo aside. "If I call the sheriff's office, can you take the responding officer back to the scene?"

"Sure thing." As Hugo passed to join his father, with lightning speed, he caught the bill of Declan's cap and flipped it off his head. "Gotcha again."

A childish game was not what he needed from his brother. Then he realized Lainey saw Hugo get the better of him. Add embarrassment on top of frustration, not to mention an overload of adrenaline he couldn't seem to release. His heart still beat faster than normal with no relief in sight.

Leaving his hat where it landed, Declan hiked to the road, made yet another call to the local sheriff, and hovered at the edge of camp until the cruiser came down the road. Scratch that. Not one patrol car. Two. He instantly regretted having made the call. This game the perp played was not worth the manpower headed in his direction.

The male deputy from the first day, carrying his trusty tablet, exited the car. The second officer identified himself as the shift manager. "Let's catch this guy. I can't send a squad car all the way out here every day."

The man, who was about his father's age, stared him down. Instantly, the memories of his dad being disappointed in him for being a car thief rushed over him. His father hadn't been interested in his side of the story. Would this man? "Yes, sir. I would like nothing more, sir. I understand you have limited resources, sir."

Declan went on to explain that Hugo would take the officers to the location of the tarp. "Maybe he left some prints on it. If you run them, I'm hoping you'll get a hit from one of the national databases."

"This isn't the big city, son." The senior officer pushed past him and followed Hugo. The "son" comment got under his skin. Not just because tenured officers often used the term to give a tongue-lashing to rookies but because it dripped with attitude and sounded like something his father would say before grounding him. Doing his best to stay calm, he entered the camp last.

His father hollered to the officers as they walked past toward the lake. "Plenty of burgers. You're welcome to stay for supper."

Just what he didn't need, his dad spinning tails of when he was on the beat over a campfire.

Lainey approached him from behind and touched him on the arm. He nearly jumped out of his skin. There were too many bogeys for him to keep track of them all. Everyone seemed to be firing at him from all sides.

She tossed his baseball cap at him. "I'd give anything to have my brother around to tease me like that again. Hugo seems to really care for you."

Declan figured her comment was meant to ease his embarrassment. It didn't. He had no right to be flustered since all his brothers were alive. She had become an only child. What kind of halfwit was he?

Meeting Lainey had become such a mess. He wished he hadn't gotten on his boss's bad side, then volunteered to stay late to make up for it. If he hadn't taken Lainey's statement, he wouldn't be here. Would finding one silver beaver for his mom be worth this hassle? Weighing the value of the silver compared to the money he and his brothers had spent only managed to infuriate him further.

Chapter Eight

The fact that two officers showed up after Declan's last call made Lainey feel a little bit safer. What had her confused was the fact the Declan hadn't gone with his brothers and the officers to view where the shooter had left the tarp. Then later, Declan's reaction to her giving him his hat back conjured new concerns. A girl tries to do a good deed and gets a scowl in return. Well, his sour face did turn a bit sheepish. Was he embarrassed? His reaction made her fear of not being able to properly judge a guy rear its ugly head again. Right now, she couldn't read Declan at all.

Add to that, Lainey's own insecurity of being a rookie treasure hunter made her miserable. She'd hoped to have found more silver beavers—no, counted on it. But the last two long hours of searching had garnered zilch, zero, nada. Well, with Declan's constant checking of his cell and other interruptions, how could a treasure hunter concentrate?

She formed a grid in her mind around the area of the first find. Maybe that beaver was a stray, and the pile was somewhere else. If each piece of silver had scattered hither and yon ... Well, that prospect made her head hurt.

To top that off, when she opened her email, her office rent notice reminded her that she'd have to ask her parents for help to pay the bill again. The Donnovan brothers owed her a bonus payment for having found one of the beavers, and with that she'd almost be able to meet her expenses. Needing less help from her parents this month was progress. Right? The familiar guilt about becoming the only child, and therefore receiving a higher level of parental monetary support, sprinkled additional discomfort into the black cloud that currently hung over her head.

She mindlessly fidgeted with the tiny four-leaf clover earrings her brother had given her for Christmas many years earlier. Finding more silver beavers and procuring more new clients was her only hope of keeping her business afloat.

"If I'm going to be in charge of chow time tonight, then let me do it my way." Colin raised his voice at Declan, who walked away shaking his head but not saying anything.

Her stomach growled. Skipping dinner might be her saving grace from all the Donnovan family tension, but her need to eat took priority. If she'd counted correctly, there'd be eight people around the campfire for burgers. Maybe she could get away with not talking? She could scarf down her food and make up some excuse to leave all the testosterone-filled guys to enjoy each other's company.

Joan managed to help Colin patty-up the burgers without undermining his authority. Lainey's even-keeled friend had stood right beside the grill-master for more than an hour, but how could she give her bestie a heads-up about her need to be alone? Her roomie understood her better than anyone. Maybe she'd catch on and make a fast exit with her? The thought of leaving Joan with six police officers as dinner companions only cranked up her already overflowing level of guilt. She might have to tough it out, if Joan wasn't in tune with her signaling attempts.

Dusk had settled by the time Hugo, Andre, and the two lawmen made it back to camp. Lainey sat facing west—to catch the last bit of the sunset—on a huge fallen tree not far from the lake. Keeping to herself, she listened while the men discussed the scene. Too bad their features were in silhouette. She couldn't make out the details of their expressions.

"Yes, I bagged and tagged the tarp," answered the senior deputy with a sarcastic tone.

Declan acted like a dog searching for a bone. "How long will it take to process the fingerprints? You're going to run the tarp for prints, right? I bet you'll get a hit. This guy's got to have priors."

The junior deputy tried to help. "I'll do the paperwork. We've got a growing backlog. I'm not making any promises. How much longer do you think you'll be searching?"

The senior deputy cut in. "The sooner you can clear this area, the less likely I'll need to send a patrol car to this location. Again."

Lainey didn't have to see the commanding officer's face to pick up on his intended message.

Declan replied, "I've got the week off, but our budgeted fieldwork is coming to a close."

Joan had managed a seven-day vacation, and Lainey had all the time in the world. So, it all boiled down to money.

Colin cleared his throat. "I just got here today. If we keep finding silver, I'll pay for a few days. The missus will get a kick out of me being videotaped with my sons. Just like the Super-8 films we took around Christmas when they were little tikes." He chuckled. "Those were fun times."

The body language of his sons told a different story. *More days means more revenue. If I can endure the Donnovan men, I won't have to lean on my dad again for the rent.* Lainey put on her metaphorical big girl panties and straightened her posture.

"Let's eat." Colin waved everyone toward the firepit.

With the cooking complete, Declan had added more wood to the fire. Even the heightened smell of smoke wasn't a deterrent from the natural beauty around her. Orange and yellow flames danced with delight for her entertainment, a great place to center her gaze as Joan and the crew of officers gathered to eat. Under different circumstances, she might better enjoy a meal under the sparkling stars.

Andre had nailed it when he said his father had all the niceties for glamping. Hugo insisted that she and Joan sit in the bag chairs, the kind of folding canvas chair that comes with a carrying case, fashioned with a hinged tray on one arm and a cup holder on the other. Who needed a dining room table? The dancing flames kept her mind occupied while she devoured her food. Colin had a talent for cooking over an open fire. The burgers were delicious with some mix of spices that tantalized her taste buds. She and Joan even split a second helping. She'd have to ask Colin for his recipe.

Lainey almost relaxed until the senior deputy turned over a milk crate and sat beside her.

"Are you enjoying our neck of the woods?" he asked.

"Sure am. I could listen to your crickets sing all night." A coyote howled in the distance. "And I don't get to hear that sound in Columbus." She snickered, and everyone seemed to join her.

The deputy leaned in her direction. "I got this cockamamie story. If you promise not to laugh, I'll tell it to you."

For a tough guy, he seemed embarrassed. She tried not to judge. "Please do."

To her surprise, his story was about a missing treasure. She'd been down this road. The storyteller wanted her to confirm if there might be any truth to what he'd been told. If her answer was yes, then she had a prospective client to woo.

"My granddad—when he was a young boy—worked for these moonshiners in North Carolina. They paid him to run errands, and he occasionally took items used as payment to a cave for safekeeping."

Lainey interrupted. "Let me guess, those moonshiners got hauled off to jail or got knocked off by their competition, leaving the valuables hidden until this very day."

The officer drew back with a start. "That's what they say. How'd you guess?"

"Most treasures are left behind because the person who hid them can't get back to them."

The man slowly eased back onto the crate. The light of the fire illuminated the gleam in his eyes. "You don't say."

Lainey held out her cell phone to him. "Give me your email, and I'll send you a link to my website so you can see my list of services."

Once his contact info had been given, Lainey's mood improved. But she hadn't noticed that Declan had strolled behind her until his voice joined in with the others.

"Or if you know the location of the cave, you should get a metal detector and try to find the treasure yourself. That's pretty much what Lainey does," offered Declan.

The words sounded so innocent. Didn't he realize he'd put the kibosh on a possible client for her? Did he think so little of her treasure-hunting abilities? Maybe he just had it out for her. She sucked in a big gulp of air and swallowed it, her fingernails digging into her palms as her fists formed.

The officer stood. "Well, my dinner break is over. I need to check in with dispatch." He tugged on his subordinate's sleeve and pulled him toward the cruisers. "Thanks for the burger. Good eats. Much appreciated."

Lainey stayed seated as Declan escorted the officers to their cars like a consummate host. *He stabs me in the back and just waltzes away.* She shot a look in Joan's direction.

Joan seemed stunned about the recent turn of events, mouthing, "I don't know."

Lainey didn't suffer often from heartburn, but she had it now.

Colin busied himself, urging his remaining sons to eat another hamburger. Hugo and Andre acted like her side of the fire was out of their hearing range.

Was Joan the only person who understood Declan had just publicly dissed her in the worst way possible?

Geez. She hadn't found additional beavers this afternoon, but there was still time. Not to mention, putting herself in harm's way to lure the hired thug out in the open distracted her more than she'd let on. Who could concentrate when she kept looking for a red laser marker on her skin and clothes? Why did Declan have to call the sheriff's office every time there was an incident? He was a cop. Was it a jurisdiction thing?

Even if she had the money for the current month's rent, if she didn't get hired again soon, she'd have to give up the lease on her office and maybe even shut down her business. Why had Declan treated her so badly?

The man was as bad as Dr. Hardy, only in a different way, and she'd kissed them both, so what did that say about her? Her lips drew into a tense straight line. She sucked at picking men. Having a romance with this cop was absolutely out of the question.

Her mind was made up. She'd look for more beavers in the morning, and if no new silver could be found, she'd pack up and go home. Taking pity money from her parents would be better than getting paid by a guy who didn't respect her intellect and skills. He'd led her on to get what he wanted just like Hardy. Both men were jerks.

* * *

It thrilled Declan to wave goodbye to the deputies. He wouldn't call them again unless he had the perp in handcuffs. Now, to get through the evening without his dad clobbering him with some veiled insult would be wonderful. If he didn't bring up topics that put them both on edge, he might have a chance. Offering to pay for a few extra search days had been mighty generous of his father. His dad loved his mother, no doubt, but was offering to pay a dig at his inability to finish something?

Since the humid breeze came out of the west, blowing east, he picked a log on the southern side of the flames. Lainey sat on the northern side, but so did his dad. Being more than an arm's length from his father gave Declan much-needed space.

"Since we have the perp's prints from the tarp, if he has any sense, he'll cut his losses and leave the area," Andre said in an overly loud voice, no doubt meant for the hired stalker to hear. If the vandal hadn't figured out that he'd left the local law a clue to his identity and still monitored the camp from within earshot, he did now. Give Andre another attaboy.

"What's the plan for tomorrow, Lainey?" If he had a confirmed schedule for tomorrow, he might get some decent shuteye tonight. Declan feared he might make some monumental blunder if he was too sleep deprived. *Making a fool of myself, caught on tape. I'd never live it down.*

Lainey stood and cleared her throat, then waited for everyone to stop talking and listen. Now she's getting all formal? Maybe she's trying to impress my dad. Good luck with that.

"Hugo, I'd like you to guard the campsite." Lainey waited for him to nod. "Andre, you video whatever you'd like. Joan and I will search the stream where the mouth meets the lake. Colin and Declan, you'll be searching upstream. Both teams will advance toward the other until they meet."

She wants me to spend the day alone with my dad? That's a hard no.

"Thanks for letting me join in on the fun part." His dad sounded pleased.

Declan waited for the other shoe to drop. Where was the "I'll find more silver than Declan" dig? He rose to stare at Lainey. The flames crackled between them. "Just a second. You and Joan will have the detector, and both know what you're doing. Dad and I, not so much. Plus, someone needs to be at your side to guard you."

"I'm leading this expedition. My word is final." Lainey rounded the fire and got in his face. "What? You can't endure spending time with your father?"

"That's not it, and you know it." Declan's blood pumped through his veins at an ever-faster pace. Why did she say that in front of his family? Was she trying to push his buttons?

"Oh, do I? Then I also know you try to get in trouble or mess things up so you can hide behind your bad-boy image."

The warmth of her breath on his face only added to the heat rising within him. Having her stab him in the back knocked him off balance. Expecting a jab from his dad, he could almost feel the air being sucked from his lungs.

"You can trash my business all you want, but I'm not letting you destroy this gift for your mother." She ended her tirade at him by poking her index finger into his chest.

Wincing, he stumbled back. Before he could regain his footing and latch onto her arm, she'd raced past him in a huff. All he could do was take in the view of her back until she ducked into her tent.

A second later, Joan offered some lame excuse and made a beeline into the tent after her.

What just happened?

"You're worse with women than I am." Hugo got up and made himself another burger.

"What's that supposed to mean?" Declan's equilibrium faltered, and he took an abrupt seat before he fell over.

"Andre gave me the impression you had a thing going with Lainey. You just destroyed it, or at the very least, you're in the doghouse."

Declan shot a glance in Andre's direction. His brother had enough sense to hide his face in the shadows. "Why does everyone think it's okay to get up in my business?"

"Now, boys, think of your mother." His dad always had to have the last word. "How about we put the bickering aside for the night? Tomorrow, we hunt for silver."

Declan's muscles were wound too tight to think about sleep. "Andre, take me to the showers or give me your keys."

"I could use a shower." Without saying another word, Andre went to his truck and rummaged around in the shopping bags.

Coming up beside him, Declan chewed on the words he wanted to say. He couldn't think of the best way to express himself and remained silent. Andre brought him a brand-new set of clothes, complete with price tags.

"Thanks." He accepted the bundle and climbed into the cab.

All the way to the public camping grounds, Andre kept his mouth shut and didn't turn on the radio. The whir of the air conditioning filled the void.

When they arrived at the showers, he picked a stall, and his little brother took the one next to him so they could share the bottle of all-in-one shampoo body wash. The washroom was dank, and the overhead fluorescent light flickered as it threatened to switch off. Maybe it was what he deserved. A cold, dark place to clean himself of his misdeeds. Declan took some of his frustration out on the plastic ties that held his new socks together. That release of energy only scratched the surface.

As he walked out into the moonlight, the inseam of his fresh-out-of-the-bag boxers chaffed his inner thigh. Added discomfort was not what he needed. He toweled off his head without much thought. It really didn't matter how his hair looked. It wasn't like he cared how his brothers, or his father, viewed him on a camping trip. He certainly didn't need to look properly groomed for Lainey. She'd told him off but good. He'd always figured he wouldn't match up to her book learning and sophistication.

"She took a cheap shot at me out of the blue, right?" He'd asked a rhetorical question. Or so he'd thought.

Andre gave him a puzzled look. "You really have no idea what you did, do you?"

"What I did?" Declan yanked the towel from his scalp. "I protected her. That's what I did."

Andre used a soft, nurturing voice in his reply. "As she tried to reel in a new client, you cut her fishing line."

Was his brother talking in metaphors? What did fishing have to do with her ripping open his old wound with his dad?

He threw his towel in the front seat of the truck. "Cut the crap and tell me what I did."

Andre sighed and strolled over to a park bench. Declan lumbered behind him and took a seat. The loud laugher of the nearby vacationers only rubbed salt into his wounds.

"Lainey owns a business. She always needs new clients. It looked like the senior deputy might hire her, then you blurted out something about getting a metal detector."

"I said that?" Declan searched his memory.

Andre's eyebrows rose. "You don't remember. Have you hit your head lately?"

"You're saying this is my fault?" Declan bent forward, dropping his view to take in loose dirt and his destroyed gym shoes.

"While you're doing some soul searching, Dad and Hugo dropped everything on a moment's notice when they thought someone had taken a shot at you. They came to protect you. It's high time you forgive Dad."

Having his little brother give him advice about romance and life had him rubbing the back of his neck and then crossing his arms. The youngest always had it the easiest. His dad hadn't been nearly as tough on him as he'd been on Hugo and himself. Maybe being able to have a good relationship with his dad made it easier for Andre to learn a few things.

Part of Declan's attraction to Lainey had come from the fact that she'd had the guts to open her own business. He wouldn't knowingly want to make her success harder to grasp. As he thought through all the things that had upset him today, if he were being honest with himself, some of them were things he'd brought upon himself.

Declan squeezed his eyes shut. "You think I should hang out with Dad tomorrow?"

An innocent punch grazed his arm. "When Lainey paired you with him, I did a little cheer in my head."

"I love you, too."

His brother yanked him off the bench and gave him a full-on hug. With his arm still around Andre's shoulder, Declan made his way back to the truck with a new respect for his younger brother.

Once seated in the cab, Declan asked, "How do I fix things with Lainey? An apology?"

His younger brother laughed out loud. Declan bit the inside of his cheek.

After a long pause, Andre broke the silence. "I don't think words will be enough. Catching the guy who's been harassing her might help."

Declan made a mental list of all the things he needed to accomplish in the next twenty-four hours to earn Lainey back.

Chapter Nine

With Colin behind the wheel and Joan in the backseat, Lainey sat in the front passenger seat as the SUV passed Andre's truck on her way to the showers. Just what she'd wanted. She'd been in the same clothes for two days but wasn't ready to see Declan again. Not tonight. Maybe a shower and some clean clothes would help her wash away the disappointment. *Why would Declan say something that could sabotage my business?*

Even the floral smell of her shampoo with revitalizing herbs didn't do the trick. The cool water didn't help. When seeing herself in the new, functional, and somehow fashionable outfit Joan had purchased for her didn't make her happy, the depths of her malaise became obvious. Sighing, she gathered her belongings and meandered out of the bathhouse.

"Lainey, over here." Colin called out to her. "I didn't know how much I smelled like smoke from making the burgers until I stuffed my dirty clothes into the plastic bag. I hope my SUV doesn't stink."

She managed to reply with a half-hearted smile. "I'm sure it's not as bad as you think."

Colin inched up close to her before whispering, "Sorry about what Declan said. His mind must have been somewhere else."

Did everybody catch Declan's faux paus except Declan? As an owl hooted off in the distance, she gave Colin a quick nod. "The fact that you and Hugo dropped everything to come help him made Declan feel good. Even if he didn't say it."

"Thanks. He got that from me. Not describing feelings with words." Colin's gaze skirted to where a row of campers stood.

A cloud glided away from the moon and the increasing brightness cleared a bit of her discontent. The would-be romance between Declan and herself might never recover, but at least she could help him patch things up with his father. "Why didn't you help him with the detective work after the accusation all those years ago? Believing a coworker's made-up story is one thing, but Declan told me he had to do all the detective work to clear his name."

"I didn't know he had a plan and put it in motion himself." Colin's body stiffened, and the grimace on his face looked menacing.

At the risk of going too far over the line, she continued. "You don't have to get defensive with me. I had nothing to do with it."

"Now wait just a doggone minute," barked Colin.

Lainey put her hand up, so that he wouldn't launch into a long tirade. She looked to see if Joan was in earshot. "I'm going to stay out of it. Please remember one thing: you were the adult, the parent. Declan was sixteen, still a kid. After the accusation, he needed you to spend time with him. To be there for him."

"You think you're an expert." Colin looked as if he wanted to walk away.

"No." She blocked his exit. "When I was about his age, my brother died in an accident. Both my parents clung to me, smothered me. Now, I look back on it, and I'm eternally grateful. I needed to feel their love more than ever during those dark days."

"I love all my sons."

"They know, but sometimes you have to show them anyway." She waited to see if he caught her meaning.

He gave her his back. "I can't change the past. Saying I was sorry didn't seem to be enough."

Lainey approached the situation from a different angle. "Do you think Declan is a good cop?"

"He's got good instincts. Better than some cops ever have, and he's still young."

"Have you told him that?"

"He knows."

"Are you sure about that?" She repositioned herself to look deep into his blue eyes. "Tell him. Better yet, show him."

A multitude of emotions crossed over Colin's face as he chewed on her suggestion. First shock, then understanding, and finally determination. "Tomorrow. I'll show him tomorrow."

"Good." The ache in Lainey's head eased, though the pain in her heart remained. Maybe Declan was a good guy, just not the right guy for her.

"Have you two solved the world's problems?" Joan walked up all smiles.

Lainey let loose a belly laugh, and Colin joined her.

"We're about to blow the doors off this hunt. I can feel it," Joan said.

* * *

After the best night's sleep she'd had in days, the next morning Lainey focused on her business. *I'll find the silver beavers and then maybe things with Declan will resolve on their own.*

The camp remained quiet throughout the morning. She drank her coffee and devoured several powdered donuts. Everyone seemed to prepare for the day based on the plan she'd laid out. Hugo cleaned and loaded his guns. Andre fiddled with his cell, playing footage he'd already captured. Colin tagged along, helping with every task Declan completed, asking questions about how to search. Joan finished up some prep work on the only metal detector still with them, exactly as Lainey had asked.

"Everybody ready? Let's find more treasure." Lainey made the announcement with confidence.

Declan hadn't made eye contact with her yet today, and he still didn't as he headed upstream, carrying a cooler. A couple of garden tools clanged together as Colin picked them up to follow his son. She let Declan leave the campsite first.

Once she could no longer see him or his father, she called out to Andre. "I'm going to start at the water's edge closest to camp. Hugo can keep an eye on me. Why don't you go get some video of Declan working together with your dad?"

Andre gave Hugo a questioning look. After receiving the nod from his oldest brother, he sprinted north to catch up.

With Hugo about fifteen feet behind her and Joan nearby, she put on her trusty headphones. She waved the wand over the water about a foot from where it lapped at the shore. This location was a good distance west from where the stream connected to the lake. Maybe Declan didn't believe the tokens could travel so far away from where the ice caves tended to form, but she had to look. That's what her father would have done. Leave no possible location unsearched.

Frank, if you're up there watching over me, guide me today. I want to make you proud.

With slow strides, she creeped along in the soft sand. In the sky overhead, a flock of birds chirped to each other as they flew past. In case she'd missed something, she retraced her steps a few feet in the dark brown silt. The beep and the bird's song sounded too similar. That's when a faint beep caught her attention. Her hiking boots would never be the same. Getting them wet again couldn't do any additional harm. As she walked straight out into the lake, the signal grew louder. She marked the spot with a long skinny branch she'd fashioned into a spear before breakfast, then took the detector back to shore.

She trudged into the lake until the waterline was thigh high, her energy renewed. So much for her new outfit. It too was about to get wet. Good thing she'd pulled her hair into a severely tight braid. That would allow her to dunk her head in and not have her curls deter her progress.

"You've got something, don't you?" Joan made a small splash as she waded in after her. "Let me hold on to you, just in case."

Her roommate grabbed hold of her belt but gave her enough slack to maneuver as she pleased. Lainey squatted in the water; her fingers followed the branch into the murky depths. Taking a deep breath, she went all the way under, scooping up as much dirt as she could hold using both hands together.

When she brought the sludge above the lake's surface, she waited for the excess water to spill out of her grasp. The stench of decaying plant life had her pulling her nose in the opposite direction. A tiny shiver went through her. Today's sunshine hadn't yet warmed the deeper water. Like a robot, she made one mechanical motion after another until she arrived at large flat rock not too far from the shore. She dumped the contents from her grasp and started sifting through it with her fingers.

Her fingernail hit something hard. She gasped and concentrated in that area of slimy mud. Sure enough, she hauled out another hard black oval and held it up for Joan.

"Yes! I'll go get the silver cleaner." Joan ran toward Andre's truck.

Elated and then terrified, Lainey shouted to her bodyguard. "More success breeds more danger. Understand?"

Hugo swung the rifle off his shoulder and used the scope to complete a quick three-hundred-sixty-degree search of the woods. "All quiet. I'll be more vigilant."

While Joan cleaned the latest find, Lainey restructured her plans to concentrate a bit deeper in the water, but she only waded in until the water came to her waist. Over the next couple of hours, she found three more for a total of five beaver tokens. Eventually, she covered an additional thirty feet without another hit and circled back to today's first recovery location. Then she headed toward the mouth of the stream and ventured north.

She'd call this hunt a success but hoped to find more. These pieces seemed to be strays. Her next likely search zone would be where pockets of deeper water pooled along the stream's edge. If they fit a logical pattern of how quarter-sized pebbles gathered, a big cluster of tokens had to be somewhere.

* * *

Without a metal detector, Declan figured Lainey just wanted to get him and his father out of her sight. He decided he'd play along until he could accomplish his goal of catching the vandal for her. Then he'd also apologize. Maybe, depending on how she acted toward him, he might ask her on a real date.

First, he had to get through the morning with his father. When a twig broke behind him, he rounded on the intruder, reaching for his pistol in its holster belted around his waist.

Andre stopped cold, then shuffled backward almost tripping over a loose rock. "I come in peace."

"A change in plans already?" Declan swiped off his ball cap and smacked it against his thigh. "Shouldn't you be guarding Lainey?"

"Hugo's got that. She's near camp." Andre held up his phone. "I'm taking videos. Act like I'm not here."

"Try to get my better side." Colin chuckled as he struck an obvious pose. "Videos. The things we Donnovan men do for your mother."

Declan remembered the one thing he had in common with his father. "You hate being photographed, too."

"Right. Let's get on with this." His father pointed upstream and started hiking in that direction again.

Having traveled further north than ever before, the landscape looked a bit different. A different species of pine tree became more prominent. The flood banks of the stream grew wider and had more curves. The force of the water that had flowed here seemed to have caused more damage to the local plant life. Now he understood what Lainey and Joan had meant when they said two-hundred years of winter thaw waters could reposition a lot of dirt.

"This looks like a good spot for a break," said Colin.

His father didn't seem out of breath, but if he needed a break then so be it. He hoped Andre would stay a good distance away. Being videoed from afar worked better for him. Taking a swig of cool water from his Thermos, he found a large boulder and claimed it as a seat.

His dad cleared his throat. "I have something I want to say to you."

Declan expected another lecture or an accusation. *I didn't plan this well enough. I've spent too much money. I need to find another profession.*

"I'd like to go on the offensive. Catch the vandal tonight after supper. You can lead the operation," his father explained with a calm demeanor.

Maybe Andre told his dad about his need to win Lainey back with actions. Going after the hired gun would take place tonight, but having his old man along might be a double-edged sword.

"You'd be okay taking orders from me?" Declan assumed the answer would be negative. He wanted to hear his father say it, anyway.

"Yes. You're a good cop. Certainly better at it than I was at your age."

Where was the back-handed compliment, the comment meant in jest? He didn't know how to respond.

"You mean you didn't know that? Me thinking you're a great cop?" His father scratched his head. "Well, son, now you do." Taking a seat beside him, Colin slapped him on the back.

Words of praise from his dad. Maybe the man had a fever. "Thanks." He still couldn't believe what had happened. If he hadn't woken up yet, this could all be a dream.

"How do you want to approach this arrest?" His dad grinned at him, apparently eagerly awaiting his next words.

Completely enthused, he grabbed a garden trowel and used it to draw a map in the damp soil at the water's edge. His father used the gardening fork as his pencil and added details to Declan's sketch. If his dad offered an idea he didn't like, he explained the cons of that idea and countered with an option of his own. To his amazement, his father worked with him, not against him. Declan approached the mission from different perspectives and decided on the best plan of attack.

"We're going to nab this guy and bring him to justice." Declan offered his father a high-five. When his dad's palm clapped with his, it was as if years of hurt melted away. He'd spent an hour with his father, and they hadn't argued. That had to be a new record.

"I guess we should dig for the silver. Lainey's already mad enough at me." Declan scratched through the etching in the dirt just in case the thief had been tailing him. As they moved farther north, the tree line inched closer to the water's edge. The heavy brush narrowed where he could stand and search. The scent of decaying wood grew stronger. Next, he went to a grouping of small rocks and hauled them out of the way. He repositioned batches of heavy debris and dug around under them.

He kept up this pattern until his cell vibrated in his pocket. He gave it a glance, thinking he'd brush off the intrusion until he realized it was a request for a FaceTime call from his mother. He immediately answered.

"Hi, Mom. What's up?" Hearing from her always made his day. Then he noticed a redness in her eyes and tracks of tears on her cheeks. "Have you been crying? What's wrong?"

His dad put his face just over Declan's shoulder and joined in on the call. "Hi, honey. Everything alright?"

"I'm fine. Don't mind me. I'm a weeping willow you know that. I'm just so happy." His mom patted under her eyes with a tissue. "Andre texted me a short video of the two of you working together. You both look so happy. I just couldn't get over it."

Andre took this opportunity to make his presence known again. "Hi, Mom. How you feeling today?"

"Not too bad." She waved.

"We've found a silver beaver. But it may be the only one." Declan wanted to lower his mom's expectations.

She smiled while more tears rolled down her face. "It's not about the silver. Seeing you genuinely happy, spending time with your dad is the biggest treasure I could ever receive."

He couldn't find the right words to respond. His father didn't seem to be doing any better.

Andre broke the silence. "I'm glad you liked the video. Wait until you see the whole show."

"Okay. I'll let you get back to work. I just wanted to be a part of the happiness." His mom blew kisses at her husband, then Andre, and finally him.

"I had no idea our situation weighed so heavily on her." Declan spoke a truth that caused him more pain than any insult his father could have levied at him.

"Saying I was sorry about the car theft wasn't enough. I should've investigated the facts myself or at the very least helped you do it. I can't undo that mistake. I hope you can forgive me." A mist welled up in his father's eye. "That chapter is closed now. Agreed?"

He pulled his dad into a bear hug. "Agreed." Not wanting to get too emotional, Declan pivoted to the evening's adventure and released the embrace as quickly as it had occurred. "Andre, I'm going to need you to stay up late with me and Dad."

* * *

The evening meal couldn't come to an end quickly enough for Declan. He'd had his father give Hugo the order to guard the camp. His responsible older brother grumbled about it but would do as requested. With Andre and his dad already collecting gear and checking the ammo in their guns, Declan decided he'd better come clean to Lainey.

"Four more silver beavers. Great work." Declan squatted next to Lainey, who sat in a bag chair near the fire.

Lainey stared at the flames. "Just doing my job."

Gosh, this is hard, but I've got to fix this. She's a good woman I want to get to know better. "About that. Nothing I could say can make up for my error with the senior deputy. I have a thousand excuses for my thoughtless comment."

Finally, she turned to look at him. His heart skipped a beat. Even as justifiable anger at him showed on her face, her beauty in the firelight was beyond anything he'd seen.

"I'll post a rave review on your website and send the link to him," he hurried on. At the risk of her yanking it away, he reached out and took her hand in his. "Tonight, Andre, Dad, and I are going after the guy who's been hired to scare you. Giving you justice is my best way of showing you how sorry I am." Swallowing hard, he'd come to the end of his rehearsed speech. Since she hadn't rejected him, he gave her hand a squeeze.

Lainey leaned toward him. "Don't get yourself killed on my account."

"If he wanted to hurt any one of us, I think he already would have. I'm not concerned about that." He kissed her cheek and stood. "Hugo will stay behind to protect you and Joan."

Now he needed to back up his words with actions. Striding with intention, he shouted, "Ready, Dad?"

His father and Andre appeared from behind Andre's truck wearing their police issued bulletproof vests. His little brother gave him all the gear he had with him that might help in capturing the perp. "Ready."

If the thug wasn't currently monitoring the camp, he and his unit had a chance to get a jump on the guy. With about thirty minutes of daylight left, he hiked as quickly as he could to the point where Lainey had shown him the footprints that veered into the bushes past the original campsite. His father took a path to his right and Andre to his left. His goal was to get past the thief's camp and come at him in a triangle formation.

He tightened the Velcro on his vest and took the safety off his gun. This guy had fired a shot over his head. He may have better aim when cornered. Too bad Declan didn't have a taser with him. He didn't want to have to fire his service weapon in the line of duty. Stealth and patience would be the key. Shielding his phone's backlight with his body as best as he could, he used his compass app to head north. By the time he could hear the waves of the intercoastal waterway between the island and Canada, the sun had set. His eyes were well adjusted to what little light the moon provided.

He went down on one knee and sent a group text to his father and Andre.

Declan: I'm in position.

Both of his fellow officers confirmed the same. Now, he waited and listened. If the vandal had stuck around after having made the mistake of leaving his tarp behind, the hope was he or one of his family would hear him. Perhaps the stalker would need a middle of the night restroom break or snore or something.

What he got was even better. The glow of a lantern became obvious. Declan figured the man had it sitting next to him on the ground. He sent another message to the group.

Declan: See the light?
Andre: Yep.
Dad: Roger that.

Declan: I'll approach. Be ready. He may know we're coming.

He took a deep breath to steady his nerves and crept toward the lamp.

When he was twenty feet away, he shouted, "Hey, buddy. I'm lost. Got any water?"

The brightness of the lantern flickered and went out. Declan stopped, belly crawled a few feet in scratchy, low grass, and continued toward the perp's position.

"Go away. I'm armed." The man's voice didn't sound too convincing.

His dad gave a bird call that sounded like a goose. He'd taught it to Declan when he was a child. Andre responded with his attempt at the same sound. It gave Declan courage. "Police! You're surrounded. Drop your weapon."

Declan popped to his feet and activated a road emergency flair Andre had given him, flinging it in the man's direction. The guy had a rifle aimed right at him. His every muscle tensed.

"Lower your gun, and we won't shoot," yelled Declan. He caught a glimpse of the reflective tape on his father's vest coming up from behind the small, vinyl tent.

"Drop it. Shooting a cop wouldn't be good for you." Leave it to Andre to try to reason with a criminal.

His dad hollered in a gruff voice. "I'll put a bullet in you before I let you shoot my son."

That got the man's attention. "It's not loaded, I swear." He dropped the rifle, fell to his knees, and clasped his hands behind his head.

This guy's been arrested before. He knows how to act. Declan continued his approach and cuffed the guy, confirming the tight grip of the smooth metal. Andre read him his rights.

With the hired gun disarmed and contained, Declan put the safety back on his pistol, holstered it, then began to look around. There were several tarps covering piles. "Is that our stuff?"

"I was going to give it back," sneered the man.

"Save it. You took a shot at me. You're going to jail." Declan's anger over the fear this man had caused Lainey spilled out with every word he uttered.

Andre's calm voice gave him pause. "Who hired you? Hardy?"

The man's head swiveled toward Andre. "I don't know the guy's name. He's paying me by the day in cash."

"Do you know what the guy who hired you looks like?" Declan's dad joined in the interrogation.

"No. Different people bring cash to my house. I got laid off, and my kid is sick." The man sat back on his heels.

Declan took control of the situation. "Do you have ID?"

"My back pocket." The perp stuck his right butt cheek toward Declan.

Fishing out the guy's wallet, he couldn't help but get a whiff of the man. He hadn't been anywhere near a shower in days. That's when he also noticed the guy's cap had an Army insignia. "You military or did you buy that at surplus?"

"I'm a vet. Look, I'd never hurt that girl. I got paid to scare her."

"You broke the window of my truck and stole our stuff." Andre came at the man, must have gotten a nose full and backed up again.

The perp's shoulders slumped. "I got a bonus for that. Like I said, I need the money."

Declan rummaged through the wallet and pulled out a Michigan driver's license. "This your current address?"

"Yeah." The defiance of the man had dwindled to a whisper.

Using his phone, Declan took a picture of both sides of the ID. Then he motioned for his team to follow him. A few feet away, he asked, "You believing this story?"

His father and brother gave him a nod.

"It's a tough situation," Dad said, "but you can't accept money to break the law and get away with it. We have laws for a reason."

"Let's have the deputy pick him up," added Andre.

At least this time the criminal was in custody and ready for processing. "I'll call the local law one more time."

Chapter Ten

Lainey twiddled her thumbs by the campfire. What was taking so long? It had been hours. The second campsite was closer to the lake and a fifteen-minute hike farther south from the site that had been vandalized. She hadn't seen or heard any signs of a commotion. She did hear the engines of a few cars as they drove past on the main road, but that could be locals or other tourists. Perhaps no news was good news, or maybe the thief wasn't anywhere close enough to be found. She thought about texting Declan, but he needed to focus.

Joan sat nearby, staring into the flames. No quick-witted quip. Her silence made the waiting that much more unbearable. Lainey'd had enough. There must be something she could do to occupy her thoughts.

On a whim, she got her tablet from her tent and brought it back to the bag chair she'd been using since Colin had arrived. Just in case someone had filled out her form requesting a consultation for her services, she logged on to her website. It stunned and elated her to see a message in her inbox. She doubted the senior deputy had any interest in hiring her after the comment made by Declan.

When she viewed the name connected to the message, she nearly passed out. Everything in her world began to spin. Dr. Mitch Hardy. *He wouldn't dare. What new type of torment is this?*

Hi Lainey:

A memory of our good times finding the jewels in Bermuda just passed through my mind. I hope your treasure hunting business is doing well. Let's keep in touch.

Pleasant regards,

Mitch

"You creep," she shouted, her voice ragged with terror. Her fingers trembled so much she almost dropped the tablet.

Joan jumped to her feet, and Hugo came running.

"I'm fine. Sorry, nothing to see here." Heat grew on her cheeks, and it had nothing to do with the firepit. *Get a hold of yourself. Don't let Hardy get to you.*

She thrust her tablet at Joan and scrutinized her reaction. Her friend, equally outraged by the message, threw the tablet onto an empty chair like it

119

carried the plague. "He has some nerve. Did you see it? He used his own email, not some made-up, untraceable throwaway." Joan walked around the pit and shook herself as if she flung off unpleasant insects or small outdoor critters.

Hugo came to her side. "Want to clue me in? Should I request that an APB be issued?"

Lainey slumped back down on the flimsy canvas chair and curled into a ball. Making herself small didn't help, but she couldn't stop from wanting to hide. "Hardy is smart enough not to incriminate himself, but thanks for the offer."

"Sure thing. I'm at your service." Hugo gave a quick look around and began his patrol again.

Just then, a rustling in the brush had the hair on Lainey's neck standing on end.

Hugo aimed his rifle at the sound. "Identify yourself."

His deep, barking voice made her flinch. Ducking below the top of the chair, she cowered.

"Stand down. It's Andre, dad, and me." Declan's voice boomed in the quiet.

Trying to tell from the tone of Declan's voice if it was good or bad news, she couldn't decide. Unfurling, she stood on shaky legs. Her breath caught as she asked, "How'd it go?"

The three silhouettes visualized into flesh and blood as the men drew closer to the fire. Each of them carried something. More than she remembered they'd had when they left.

Declan came up to her, giving her a long, hard, rectangular case. "I think this belongs to you."

"My metal detector," she squealed and grabbed the warm handle from him. "Is it okay? Are you okay? Did you find the guy?" As she approached him, she viewed the dark stains on his pants and the smell of grassy mud grew.

Colin interjected with a satisfied grin, "Declan found the suspect and cuffed him with an assist from Andre and myself. The hired gun is now in the custody of the sheriff awaiting arraignment." He gave a little bow.

"We can all sleep a bit easier now. I don't think Hardy can hire a replacement hitman and get him out here tonight." Andre gave Joan her suitcase.

LAINEY SHEA'S TREASURE QUEST: THE SILVER BEAVER TOKENS

Joan showed Declan the message on Lainey's website. His eyebrows pulled together. "The time stamp on this message is right before we cornered the perp. Maybe he got off a distress signal before we captured him. It won't stand up in court, but I don't think that's a coincidence."

* * *

Early the next morning, after breakfast, Colin guarded the camp while Lainey and everyone else hiked to the thief's hideout. It took all five of them to carry back everything that had been stolen.

"So, we lost most of the food, but all my equipment and other tools have been recovered. I'll give you a discount to match anything Andre's insurance didn't cover on his truck." Lainey noticed all the Donnovan men shaking their heads, but she'd find a way to make them whole anyway. It was the right thing to do. She always paid her debts.

Picking up a satchel of digging tools and her recently recovered detector, she yelled at the top of her lungs, "Let's go find the rest of the silver!"

Colin hung close to camp, while Andre and Joan used a metal detector on the south end of the stream. Hugo tagged along with Declan and Lainey. The oldest sibling seemed enthused that he finally got to do more than stand guard.

"Because we found one beaver here and there, it tells me that occasionally the current was strong enough to carry one away from the pile. This gives me hope that we may be able to find a big grouping together." She took long strides to keep pace with the men until she reached the most northly point on her trip.

"What should I look for?" asked Hugo.

"I'm going to search for big bends in the stream with lots of debris. My guess is that's what's keeping most of the silver in place."

Lainey enjoyed the sun on her face and the cloudless sky. The tops of the trees softly waved back and forth. The low humidity made it a good hair day, and that pleased her beyond words. She'd waved her wand over several batches of fallen branches but didn't get a hit.

"Look up ahead. That's a big pile." Declan pointed toward Canada.

It absolutely piqued her interest. "Oh, that pile of logs is so big. I don't think the three of us are going to be able to roll them out of the water on our own."

Declan hauled out his cell and called his father. "Hey, Dad. We need all of us together. Keep coming upstream until you find us."

Lainey picked up medium-sized branches as Declan and Hugo worked in unison to clear bigger logs. Occasionally, she passed the detector over the area. She kept hearing a faint beep in one spot but didn't want to get too excited. It could be a pile of aluminum cans.

When the trio arrived, she gave the order to have all of them on one side of the last huge fallen tree. "Roll this trunk a good foot or more west."

Even with the six of them giving it their all, the waterlogged wood didn't budge. "Scrape the dirt away from the dry side. We must break the suction between the water and the mud."

Using garden tools and her professional archeology dig equipment, it took a good hour to free the tree from the grasp of the warm mud. Lainey called for a break, and Andre used the camera's timer to take a quick picture of the whole group standing by the dig site. She enjoyed this day so much more, knowing the hired thug couldn't hurt her, although with so much activity the night before and this morning, she hadn't had a chance to have a private word with Declan.

Every time she snuck a glance in his direction, she almost always caught him keeping tabs on her. She'd smile, and he'd grin back at her. Neither shied away from the fact that, with the danger temporarily at bay, the sparks between them rekindled. Her behavior toward him reminded her of when she had a crush in high school. She reveled in the feeling. He'd kept her safe and had promised to try to undo the damage his comment may have caused. Not to mention, Declan getting along with his father made Declan a much happier guy to be around. Maybe after Declan was no longer a client, their relationship could progress into a new phase.

With the break over, Lainey lined everyone up, putting Hugo, Declan, and Andre at the broadest portion of the trunk. "On three." She counted it down and with them all pushing, the trunk began to lift out of the water. With one final push, and a great deal of cracking of the smaller branches, the tree rolled clear of the silt that had encased it onto the grassy shore. The newly released mold and mildew that reached her nose was so strong she could almost taste it.

Lainey grabbed one wand and Joan the other. As both advanced toward the middle, the machines gave off their tell-tale signs of metal detected. She wasn't sure who hollered first, but the six of them made a great deal of commotion.

LAINEY SHEA'S TREASURE QUEST: THE SILVER BEAVER TOKENS

Lainey shouted over the din, "Let's be systematic about this." Everyone fell silent, except for a nearby squirrel that had scurried up a tree. "There's a process to digging. I'll do it."

The frowns on the faces of the men almost made her laugh. Joan, in contrast, opened her tool kit and began laying them out atop the log they'd pushed back out of the water. Luckily, the beeps took place in the soft mud under where the tree had been shifted onto less waterlogged land. In the summer, the depth of the stream was low. Lainey took her time and had asked Andre to video the dig for posterity and Declan's mom. Within thirty minutes, she'd extracted about a foot of dirt but kept samples in plastic bags every three or four inches. Eventually, she hit something very hard. The cold soil turned very black. She dislodged what she decided could have been the remnants of a fur pouch and saved that, too.

One by one, she extracted oval-shaped pieces. Thirty-seven in all. Joan laid them out on a red blanket in the sun on the opposite side of the stream. Andre repeatedly came up behind Lainey and stuck the camera in her face. She got used to it. Even with no makeup, she didn't care what she looked like. The silver beaver tokens were the stars.

With a sigh, she washed her hands in the stream and asked Joan to get the detectors for one final pass. She waved the wand, and Joan did the same behind her. She rescanned every inch of dirt on the bend where the debris had been the heaviest. No more beeps.

"Well, we found all of them from this location. That makes forty-two so far. There might be a couple more strays between here and the lake. Should we keep looking?" Lainey asked an honest question. Keeping the client happy was the main goal of her business, after all.

To her surprise, Colin gave her a round of applause and all his sons joined him. That made her day. She could get used to finding treasures. A big gust of wind bent the trees overhead. It made her think of her brother, Frank. She'd continue to keep her promise to him.

When she asked Joan to help her gather her tools, Declan instead tugged at her arm and pulled her aside.

"Before we get interrupted again, I want to ask. Would you like to go to the Columbus Zoo and have dinner with me?" The cutest expression came onto his face. A bit of shyness and a whole bunch of manliness.

"I'm so happy you asked." Without thinking much about it, she threw her arms around his neck. He grabbed her middle and lifted her high above his head, putting her in the same position she'd been in when she'd first kissed him.

When she looked down at his attractive, dimpled face, he planted a swoonworthy kiss on her lips. She kissed him back with equal passion. Even knowing she had an audience and a camera lens pointed in her direction, she didn't care. Declan had proven himself to be a good guy. A capable man and a worthy boyfriend. Maybe her ability to read men had come back online. She trusted herself, and she trusted him. She gave him another lengthy, tender smooch.

* * *

A month later, at her condo, Declan pulled her on top of his lap as they sat on her couch in her modestly furnished condo. Joan had made some excuse to go to the library to complete a research project, giving her the place to herself and the man she couldn't do without. She reminisced about all the wonderful things that had happened in the past few weeks.

A week after they'd returned from the treasure hunt, Declan picked her up to go to the Columbus Zoo. She'd only seen him in his uniform and jean shorts, so when he came in dress pants and a pressed pale blue shirt, she took notice. The man cleaned up well. The vibe between them had changed. He was no longer her client, and maybe he acted more relaxed around her because she wasn't in professional mode. The date went well, and the physical chemistry between them couldn't be denied.

Two weeks ago, the Donnovan family had invited her and Joan to see the unveiling of Andre's treasure hunt video. Colin had even invited her parents. Both sets of parents had enjoyed each other's company before she and her parents had moved away, and when they got back together, it was like no time had passed. The footage was funny and heartwarming. Seeing herself in work mode was hard. She decided she needed to lighten up. Maybe the courage to do so would come with experience.

Last week was quite the whirlwind. The Hudson's Bay Company History Foundation had invited her for an unveiling of her find as part of their authentication process. The Donnovan family graciously allowed her to take all the silver beaver tokens to temporarily be on display. At this press conference, she spoke on behalf of her Lainey Shea's Treasure Quest Company. No one else had asked to get credit or have time to speak. The spotlight was all hers, and she soaked it in. Hopefully, the critical success of the historical find would translate into more paying customers.

Declan received a copy of the background check the Michigan police did on the guy hired to harass her. He had no prior dealings with the law, and his former employer confirmed the date that his job had been eliminated. She assumed the line about having a sick child was also true. Taking the advice of the Donnovan cops, she listed the value of the stolen items to be worth less than a thousand dollars. The man was then convicted of a misdemeanor and sentenced to one year in jail and a two thousand dollar fine. She could have gone for a felony conviction but hoped this bad experience would teach him that breaking the law was never the answer to financial problems.

Of course, there was no way to officially connect Dr. Mitch Hardy to the hired thug. The instances of her tire being slashed or random messages on her website stopped, but the uneasy feeling she had about the whole situation never went away. Lainey kept her guard up in case Hardy decided to regroup and try again. It gave her great peace of mind that Declan had installed security cameras around her condo. He went with her to self-defense classes. When she was with him, a sense of safety resonated in her bones. Still, she couldn't help looking over her shoulder often when she was alone.

Today, Declan had said he needed to study for his detective's exam. His books were on her coffee table, and she was instead on his lap. "I've got work to do. Aren't you supposed to be studying?"

He rolled his eyes. "Yes, but I can think of something much more invigorating." Nuzzling his nose against hers, he waggled his eyebrows and looked toward her bedroom.

"Business before pleasure." She managed to slide off his lap, even though he tried to stop her hasty exit. Giggling, she tossed him his book, and he sighed.

On the opposite side of her brown leather couch, she opened her tablet and logged in to her website. Seeing the wonderfully complimentary recommendation he'd written for her made her smile every time she got a glimpse of it. Andre had gotten a fabulous picture of her when Declan had lifted her into the air on the last day of the hunt. Having that picture next to the one of her with all the tokens at the press conference in Canada was a nice way to gain clients.

Among the inquiries about her services, she recognized the name of the senior deputy. He'd signed her contract and said he'd wire her a deposit. "Declan. The deputy from Michigan hired me."

A broad smile spread across his face. "I'm a man of my word. I told you I'd explain that I wasn't thinking straight at the campfire. You deserve his business. You've earned it."

It was in that moment that she decided she'd never lost her ability to judge men. Hardy was a conniving oaf. Now, she could better spot men who were ingenuine. She could trust most men, and she could definitely trust Declan.

Swiping his book from him, she pitched it on the table, grabbed his shirt, and led him behind a closed door. Every part of her life was on an upswing, and she planned to savor it to the fullest.

"You're the treasure I've been hunting for, and I want you all to myself," she said as she pulled him into a warm embrace.

THE END

ABOUT VICKEY WOLLAN

Always a rambunctious child, Vickey Wollan brings that energy and curiosity to her sweet adventure romance writing. Travel along as her archaeologist heroine, Laney Shea, takes you with her into the wilderness and beyond finding hidden treasures a plenty.

Lainey is book and street smart but often finds herself in dangerous situations. Luckily, she attracts many kinds of heroes to assist her in her arduous quests. As an entrepreneur, she must always fulfill her client's dreams by finding the treasures they seek.

In addition to adventures, Vickey's original works have Christmas themes because she likes to keep her inner child alive. Whether it is her three-novel series: *A Snowflake Christmas – The Series* set in a mountainous small town or her short stories in *A Cheery Christmas Collection*, these tales can best be described as festive, wholesome, and heartwarming.

Vickey lives in Florida with her business partner-husband. Together they've traveled to many countries and a great deal of America's National Parks. Hiking the outdoors is a great way to allow one's imagination to run free. Those experiences fuel her creativity as she plots her next story.

Thank you for your curiosity and interest in Vickey Wollan's creations. Please check back often for her most recent story that will transport you on an adventure.

For a complete list of her published works, visit her website vickeywollanauthor.com.

OTHER BOOKS BY VICKEY

Her sweet, small town, Christmas themed romance books include:

A Snowflake Christmas

A Snowflake Christmas - The Nutcracker

A Snowflake Christmas - The Elf

A Snowflake Christmas - The Series

A Cheery Christmas Collection

She has also written short romance stories for these **First Coast Romance Writers** anthologies:

Romancing the Holidays - An Elf's Challenge

Romancing the Holidays - Volume 2 - The Secret Santa Surprise

Romancing the Holidays - Volume 3 - A Boat Built for Two

Romancing the Tropics - Baubles in Bermuda

Visit her website vickeywollanauthor.com to learn more and for links to your favorite retailers.

CONNECT WITH VICKEY

If you liked Lainey Shea's Treasure Quest - The Silver Beaver Tokens, she would greatly appreciate it if you left a kind review at the retailer's website.

Sign up for her newsletter and get a FREE short story. Visit her website vickeywollanauthor.com to sign up.

Here are her social media links: She would love to hear from you.

Facebook
vickeywollanauthor

Goodreads
Vickey_Wollan

Website
Vickey Wollan Author

X
authorvickey

BookBub
vickey-wollan

Instagram
authorvickeywollan

Newsletter

TikTok
@vickeywollanauthor

Milton Keynes UK
Ingram Content Group UK Ltd.
UKHW021909020524
442050UK00014B/544

9 798224 502929